Pinal Ariz

Resources of Pinal County, Arizona

Pinal Ariz

Resources of Pinal County, Arizona

ISBN/EAN: 9783742815644

Manufactured in Europe, USA, Canada, Australia, Japa

Cover: Foto ©Andreas Hilbeck / pixelio.de

Manufactured and distributed by brebook publishing software
(www.brebook.com)

Pinal Ariz

Resources of Pinal County, Arizona

CORREGGIO,

AND

PARMEGIANO.

SKETCHES

OF THE

LIVES

OF

CORREGGIO,

AND

PARMEGIANO.

LONDON:

PRINTED FOR LONGMAN, HURST, REES,
ORME, BROWN, AND GREEN.

1823.

ADVERTISEMENT.

———

THE original materials for these Sketches were collected at Parma and Rome, during a short excursion into Italy, in 1785 and 1786. They were subsequently communicated to several artists of eminence, and different persons conversant in the fine arts, who, like the writer, were sensible of the errors and defects which prevailed in the printed accounts of Correggio and Parmegiano, published in this country. A diffidence of his own knowledge of painting, however, prevented him from giving them to the public, and he conceived, that as the materials were principally drawn from the works of Ratti, Tiraboschi, and Affò, they would not long remain unknown to the English reader. But as several years elapsed, without any material correction of the errors,* which disfigured our biographical accounts of these two painters, the undertaking was resumed, at the suggestion of persons eminent in the art, and the outline has been en-

* We must except from this remark the brief notices in James's work on the Italian schools of painting; West's Lectures, contained in Galt's account of his life; and Bryan's Dictionary of Painters. But these works, from their very nature, cannot admit those details, which are requisite to satisfy the inquisitive Reader.

larged and corrected, by a perusal of
works of later date, printed abroad,
of which an account will be given
in the Introductory Observations.
Although these Sketches have been
some time finished for the press, the
author still suspended the publication,
under the impression that the task
would be satisfactorily performed by
some other hand, particularly since
the researches of Pungileoni, the
latest biographer of Correggio, have
brought so many valuable documents
to light.   But finding that no one has
yet availed himself of these advantages, he submits with diffidence these
Sketches to the English reader, from a
hope that many parts will at least
possess the attraction of novelty.

Several of the notes and illustrations being too long to be conveniently subjoined to the text, will be found at the end of each chapter, according to their respective references.

June 25, 1823.

For the Head prefixed to this work, and
mentioned in the third chapter, p. 194, the writer
is indebted to the kindness of John Jackson,
esq. R. A., who copied it from a portrait near
the door of the cathedral at Parma, considered
as that of Correggio.

*Denominations, and Value of the Foreign Coins
mentioned in this Work.*

IN these pages the foreign denominations
of money are retained; for it would be difficult to reduce the different sums mentioned to
the English standard, without conveying a
false impression; the relative value of money in
different countries, and different ages, being too
variable to be subjected to any accurate criterion. We shall, therefore, only observe,
that the gold ducat, so frequently mentioned,
is rated by Tiraboschi as equal to a Venetian Zecchine; which varied in value according to the price of gold, from 9*s.* 6*d.* to
10*s.* 6*d.*, and therefore its average value is
10 shillings. Its positive value at the time of
Correggio, may be estimated, by the consideration, that an acre of land sold for about ten
of these ducats; and consequently that, according to the prices of this country, it was worth
at least six times its nominal amount, at the
present day.

The scudo d'oro or gold crown was an imaginary coin, equal to about 7*s*. 6*d*. sterling, and the Roman current crown to 5*s*. bearing a similar proportion to our present money.

The lira was also imaginary, and appears to have been subjected to a trifling variation, at different times and places, as is shewn by the following records of payments, made to Correggio, for his works at Parma, wherein in one instance the ducat is rated at 5 lire imperiale, and in the other at about 5¼.

Item il soprascritto pittore debe fare lire cento imperiali videl. ducati *vinti* d'oro a lui numerati, &c.   Pungileoni, t. ii, p. 170.

" Habuisse et recepisse ducatos septuaginta sex auri et in auro et sol. tredecim imp. pro completa solutione ducator. ducent. septuag. qnq. auri et in auro largos, in rationem *librar. quinque et sol. septem* pro singulo ducato, &c." Ib. p. 201.

Hence the imperial lire mentioned in these pages, may be rated according to the value of the ducat, at about 2 shillings of English money.

It is also necessary to observe, that some authors have been led into an erroneous estimate of the prices paid to Correggio, by grounding their calculation on the value of the common or modern lira, which is rated in different parts of Italy at from 6d. to 8½d.

See also Tiraboschi, t. vi, p. 266.

GENEALOGICAL TABLE of the FAMILY of ALLEGRI.

Antonio,
living about 1400.

Giacomo,
ment. 4 May, 1445.

Antonio = Francesca Canroni,
testamenti   di Tolano.
dated in
1465.

Christoforo,
m.
Orsolina Affaroi
di Correggio.

Baldesarre.

Marco.

Lorenzo Pittore.
m.
1. Caterina Calcagni.
2. Maria Prato.
d. 1527.

Giovanni.

Elisabetta.

Bernardino.

Pellegrino, = Bernardina
d. 1546   Aromani, di
                 Correggio.

Caterina,
m. Vincenzo Mariani.

ANTONIO, = Girolamo Martini.
b. 1493 or 4.   b. 1505.
d. 1534.

Pomponio Quirino, = Laura Genitaluni
b. 1541.   di Correggio.
living 1596.

Francesca Lelola,
m. Pomponio Brunorio,
b. 1594.

Caterina,
died young,
b. 1546.

Anna Geria,
died young,
b. 1527.

Girolamo Caterina.

Pompilio.

Antonio Pellegrino
Pittore,
d. 1591.

Sulpizia.

Sertima Elisabetta.

CORREGGIO.

BIOGRAPHICAL SKETCH

OF

ANTONIO DE' ALLEGRI,

SURNAMED

CORREGGIO.

INTRODUCTORY

OBSERVATIONS.

THE accounts delivered to posterity concerning the family and life of
the celebrated Correggio, were long
extremely scanty and uncertain. His
life published by Vasari, in the " Vite
de' piu eccellenti Pittori, Scultori, ed
Architetti," is full of errors and incon-
sistencies; while many subsequent
authors did little more than copy this

superficial narrative, and disfigure it
with additional inaccuracies.

Hence have arisen the most con-
tradictory and discordant opinions.
Some writers consider Correggio as
descended from an obscure family,
and living in indigence; they repre-
sent him as vending his works at a
low price, and occasionally descend-
ing to paint signs for apothecaries
and inn-keepers, and the portraits
of persons of mean condition.

Others, on the contrary, derive his
origin from the illustrious family, who
were distinguished in the fourteenth
and fifteenth centuries, as Princes of
Correggio. They suppose him pos-

sessed of considerable property, and have conferred on him a shield of arms, in which the horse, deemed a proof of nobility, is the chief bearing.

Not only his lineage, but even the time of his birth and death have been differently represented. Vasari records the period of neither, and dates his principal works about 1512, when he had scarcely attained his nineteenth year.

According to some, Correggio is represented as having received a classical education, and as intimately versed in sculpture, architecture, mathematics, and philosophy; an

assertion which has been as strenuously denied by others, and all his
excellence attributed solely to the
efforts of native genius, which,
without a preceptor, and deprived
of the advantages of a liberal education, supplied those deficiencies
from the resources of the mind.

Pages are written on one side, to
prove that he passed his whole life
at Correggio and Parma, and never
saw the master-pieces of his con-
temporaries; and, on the other, no
less arduous efforts are made, to shew
that he visited Rome and Florence,
and caught a sudden spark of inspi-
ration from the works of Raphael
and Michael Angelo.

Some of these erroneous conjectures were first corrected by his admirer Mengs, in the series of Treatises intitled : " Considerations on the Design, Chiaro Scuro, Colouring, Composition, Drapery, and Harmony, of Raphael, Correggio, and Titian"— " Taste, Design, Chiaro Scuro, Colouring, Composition, Ideal, of Correggio "—" Memoirs concerning the Life and Works of Antonio Allegri, denominated Correggio"—and " Reflections upon the Excellence of Correggio." These tracts were translated from the original Italian into English, and published in three volumes, in 1796. Some additional corrections and notices were furnished by Ratti, the echo of Mengs, in

a work intitled "Notizie Storiche sin-
cere, intorno la Vita e le Opere del
celebre Pittore Antonio Allegri da
Correggio," printed at Finale in 1781.
But we are still more indebted for a
further elucidation of the subject, to
the laborious investigations of the
learned Tiraboschi, ducal librarian at
Modena, who gave a sketch of the life
of this distinguished painter, in the
" Storia della Litteratura Italiana,"
and enlarged it in the 6th volume of
the " Biblioteca Modenese," published in 1786.* In these biographical
narratives, he, in numerous instances,
separated truth from falsehood, and
facts from traditional information;

---

* Article Correggio.

and although, from the scantiness of contemporary notices, and the paucity of authentic documents, some obscurity still remained, yet Tiraboschi ascertained the lineage and station of Correggio, the era of his birth and death, the places of his residence, the prices which he obtained for some of his principal works, and the chief incidents of his life. Further lights were elicited by Lanzi, in his brief, but able sketch of the life of Correggio, in the "Storia Pittorica dell' Italia." The obscurity which still remained, has finally been as much removed, as could be expected, from the distance of time, and the changes and revolutions of society, by the indefatigable researches of Signor Luigi Pungileoni, in his " Memorie Istoriche di Antonio Allegri, detto il Correggio," published at Parma in three volumes octavo, 1817, 1818, 1821.

From these authors, the foundation of the ensuing narrative is principally drawn, although we have not neglected to consult the accounts of other biographers and writers on the fine arts.

CORREGGIO.

CHAP. I.

*Birth, Parentage, and Education of Antonio
de' Allegri, surnamed Correggio—Conjectures
relative to his early Instructors in the Art of
Painting, Mantegna, Bianchi, and others—
Studies Anatomy under Doctor Lombardi—
His early Progress in his Profession—Paints
an Altar-piece for the Franciscan Convent of
Minor Friars at Correggio—Paintings executed for the Hospital of Mercy, and the
Church of St. Nicholas at Carpi ; also
the St. George, for the Church of St. Pietro
Martire, now preserved in the Gallery at
Dresden—His Marriage—Prosperous Si-
tuation of his Family—The three Pictures of
the Marriage of St. Catherine.*

ANTONIO de' Allegri, usually called
Correggio, was born in 1493, or 1494.[A]
The family from which he was des-

cended, had been long settled at Correggio, and bore the appellation of Allegri; for we find one of that name recorded in 1329, as doing homage to the princes of that city. A descendant of this man, *Giacomo*, was father to Antonio, the first of whom any distinct information can be procured, and who was living at Correggio towards the beginning of the fifteenth century. His grandson, Antonio, had by his wife, Francesca Toano, four sons, of whom two survived. Lorenzo, the younger, was a painter by profession; and the elder, Pellegrino, espoused Bernardina Piazzoli, or Aromani, by whom he had three daughters, two of whom died young, and an only son, ANTONIO, the celebrated painter, and the subject of this narrative. Antonio bore various appellations; Allegri, his family name, de Allegris, and Lætus, the synonyms in Latin, and the Italian derivative Lieto; but these, according to the custom of the time, are lost in the appellative Correggio, taken from the place of his birth.

The city of Correggio had long flourished, as the capital of an independent principality, and its sovereigns are justly commemorated as the patrons of literature and the arts. At the close of the fifteenth century, the government was jointly exercised by Manfredo, Nicolo, and Gilberto,[a] members of the same illustrious family, the last of whom was the husband of Veronica Gambara,[c] so renowned for her protection and cultivation of letters. In a city where literature and the arts were thus favoured, and their professors encouraged and patronised, the means of liberal education were not deficient ; and hence we find that Antonio was carefully instructed, under the auspices of his father, Pellegrino, a tradesman of moderate property, and, as such, entitled to the appellation of maestro or master,* then a respectable distinction.   Antonio acquired the rudiments of knowledge under Giovanni Berni, a native of Placentia, and was afterwards instructed by Battista Marastoni, a Modenese, in rhetoric, and the other branches of polite literature.

In general, the masters of persons eminent in painting are well known.

---

* Pungileoni, L. i. p. 6.

Perugino was distinguished as the
instructor of Raphael, and Bellini as
the master of Titian; but we have
no specific authority, to ascertain by
whom this paragon of the art was
taught. We have reason, however, to
conclude, that his talent for painting
was developed at an early period;
and from the tradition of his native
place, it is not unlikely that he acquired the first rudiments of design
under his uncle Lorenzo. From him,
however, he could have derived little
more than the elements of his art; for
Lorenzo was never sufficiently eminent to rescue his own name from
oblivion, and is, in fact, mentioned in
documents of the age, in terms which
would rank him as little higher than
a house-painter of the present day.
In the *Rime* of Vittoria Colonna,

printed at Bologna in 1543, the com-
mentator, Rinaldo Corsi, observes,
"Like one of our painters of Correggio,
named master Lorenzo, who, wishing
to delineate a lion, drew a goat, and
affixed to it the title of a lion."[a]

The researches of Pungileoni appear indeed to prove, that several
artists of merit flourished at this
time at Correggio. Among these he
particularly specifies Antonio Bartolotto, whose family appellation was
Ancini, but who adopted the name
of his father Bartolotto.   He is sometimes mentioned by the name of
Tonino, the diminutive of Antonio.
The only authentic specimen of his
pencil yet extant, resembles so

---

[a] Pungileoni, t. ii. p. 25.

nearly the early style of Correggio, as to justify the inference, that our young painter was either formed by his instructions, or profited by the study of his works. This painting, in fresco, exhibits a Madonna and Child, with an angel presenting a basket of cherries; St. Quirino offering a model of the town of Correggio; and St. Francis displaying his stigmata or wounds. Some branches of laurel or palm, the foreshortening of the infant's leg, and the graceful air of the heads, together with the introduction of two rabbits, partake strongly of the peculiarities of Correggio, to whose pencil this performance has even been attributed. Bartolotto is frequently mentioned in conventual registers, from 1510 to 1513, as being employed in different works by the monks, though the sums which he received were extremely small, as the highest payment specified is twenty-one lire, or four ducats.[*] The time of his birth and death is equally uncertain.

To other painters of greater celebrity the honour of instructing Correggio has also been attributed; for in the neighbourhood, two of considerable eminence, namely, Andrea Mantegna and Francesco Bianchi, were established, under whom tradition has placed our young artist.

Andrea Mantegna,[D] after studying under Squarcione, and Giacomo Bellini, the founder of the Venetian

---

[*] Pungileoni, t. ii. p. 27.

school, and after visiting Florence,
Rome, and other principal cities of
Italy, had settled at Mantua. He
was distinguished as the cultivator, if
not the inventor of foreshortening, in
which Correggio so much excelled.
Although our young painter had
scarcely reached the age of 13 before
the death of Andrea, which happened in 1506, yet, as he was a
youth of singular genius and indefatigable industry, he might have received at so early an age instructions from this celebrated master,
whose style, according to the opinion
of Mengs, Lanzi, and others, he seems
to have caught in his early productions. At all events, he might have
studied under his sons Ludovico and
Francesco, who succeeded to the
school established by their father,

and might have profited by the rich collection of models and copies, which it contained. This opinion would be strongly corroborated, could we give full credit to the statement of the Abate Lanzi, that several of Correggio's juvenile productions are still preserved at Mantua, and display the germ of future excellence, blended with the stiff and rigid style of the old school. The pictures, however, which he mentions, as attributed to Correggio, are authenticated by evidence too slight, to form a valid foundation for argument.[*]

The other painter under whom Correggio is said to have studied, was Francesco Bianchi,[e] who was distin-

---

[*] Lanzi, Storia Pittorica dell' Italia, t. vi. p. 59.

guished for his fine colouring and graceful airs, two perfections which eminently mark the works of our painter. From the vicinity of Correggio both to Mantua and Modena, and the reputation which Mantegna and Bianchi enjoyed at the time, we are inclined to assent to the opinion, which has been delivered down by tradition, that either directly or indirectly, he owed the first improvement of his great talents to these two masters. Correggio did not, however, content himself with a mere mechanical practice of his art; for his pictures display an intimate acquaintance with the principles of perspective, sculpture, and architecture, as well as with the philosophy of colours; and, above all, his knowledge of anatomy is generally recognized, in his accurate delineation of the human form. From whom he drew his acquaintance with the former sciences is unknown; but his recent biographer, Pungileoni, has enabled us to ascertain his instructor in anatomy: this was Doctor Giambattista Lombardi,[F] a native of Correggio, who had been professor at Bologna, and afterwards at Ferrara. He finally settled in his native town, as physician to Nicolo, a prince of the reigning family, towards the beginning of the 16th century, and was held by him in high consideration.

With this learned physician Correggio long continued in habits of the strictest intimacy. A manuscript, on parchment, of the Geographia of Francesco Berlingheri, in which the autograph of Lombardi appears, with the date of Feb. 1st, 1488, is supposed to have been presented by him to Antonio, on the 2nd of June, 1513, from an autograph of that date, "Antonius Allegri, die 2 de Zugno, 1513.". It is conjectured to have been a gift by Lombardi, in return for his portrait, which Correggio is said to have painted about that period. This portrait is considered by Pungileoni as that of the Physician now preserved in the Gallery of Dresden, which is much admired for the beauty of the colouring, and the expression of gravity and intelligence blended in the countenance. Their subsequent intimacy is proved, by the attendance of Lombardi as godfather at the baptism of his son Pomponio, in 1520; and as Lombardi lived

till 1524, the young painter must
have derived considerable advantage
from his extensive knowledge * in
other sciences, as well as in that of
anatomy.

Many pictures and sketches have
been commemorated, as executed by
Correggio in this early period of his
career. He is said to have painted
landscapes and other pieces, which
were sometimes given to his friends,
and sometimes sold publicly at his
native place. Among these we may
perhaps rank the curious and interesting sketch, now in the collection of
the Marquis of Stafford, and formerly
preserved in the Gallery of the Duke
of Orleans. It is slightly coloured,

---

* Pungileoni, t. i. pp. 19, 128, 170 ; t. ii. p. 51.

and represents a Muleteer conducting a loaded Mule and a Foal, and engaged in conversation with a peasant. It is supposed to have been once used as a sign to an inn, though on what authority is now unknown.

But whatever uncertainty may prevail, with regard to the instructors of Antonio, or the objects of his youthful studies, we cannot doubt that he was distinguished in his profession, before he had completed his twenty-first year; for none but eminent painters were then employed in decorating the altars of rich convents and religious houses.[G]

The sum of one hundred ducats having been bequeathed to the Franciscan Convent of Minor Friars at

Correggio, for the erection of an altar-
piece in their church, they selected
Antonio Allegri for the work; and
with the consent of his father, Pellegrino, he entered into an agreement[k]
for the purpose, on the 30th of August,
1514. The price stipulated was one
hundred ducats, of which fifty were
paid in advance, exclusive of the wood,
which was provided by the community,
at the expense of twenty-two ducats
more. Ten ducats were also assigned
for leaf gold, besides the charge
for erecting the scaffolding and other
preparations. This sum, as his recent
biographers justly argue, indicates no
ordinary degree of reputation, and
completely refutes the idle assertions
of Vasari and his superficial copyists,
that Correggio was ill paid for his
works; since such a recompence,

according to the comparative value
of money, would be deemed a liberal
reward, for so young an artist, even
at the present day.

This altar-piece represented the
Virgin, supporting the infant Saviour
in her lap, with St. Joseph on one
side, and on the other St. Francis,
kneeling. The height was 2 braccia,
and the breadth 1¾, or nearly 5 feet
by 4. The painting remained in its
place until August, 1638, when it was
stolen, and an inferior performance
substituted, as was supposed, by a
Spanish painter, who, by the permission of the governor, Annibale Molza,
was suffered to take a copy.

The loss of so valuable a piece was
regarded as a public calamity, and

almost occasioned a commotion; for after the convocation of a general council, above two hundred persons of all ranks assembled in the anti-chamber of the governor's palace, to complain of the robbery, and demand justice on the offenders. A deputation of nobles was also sent to the Duke of Modena and to the Bishop·of Reggio, for permission to prosecute the Friars, who had connived at the theft. Memorials were presented to the Pope, to the sacred college, and to the general and provincial of the order; but all these efforts were ineffectual, and no traces of the original have been since discovered. *

Another proof of early eminence is

---

* From documents quoted by Tiraboschi.

a piece, which he probably painted about the same period, for the brotherhood of Santa Maria, or the Hospital of Mercy, at Correggio. It is described as an altar-piece, in three compartments, of which the centre represented God the Father, and the two others, St. John and St. Bartholomew. This painting was purchased, in 1612, by Giovanni Siro, the last prince of Correggio,[1] at the price of three hundred ducatoons, and is either lost, or has passed into obscure hands.*

As these pictures are both lost, we have no means of comparing the style of his early pencil with that of his later years, except from a

---

* Pungileoni, t. ii. pp. 82, 83, where the documents relative to the sale of the picture are printed.

piece, which is now preserved in the
gallery of Dresden, and which Mengs
conjectures to have been painted about
this period of his life, as an altar-
piece for a chapel, in the church of
St. Nicholas, at Carpi. Here he is
supposed to have been in 1512, from a
deed in which an Antonio Correggio
appears as a witness.[k] It represented
the Virgin and Child sitting on a kind
of throne, under a canopy of the Ionic
order, with the figures of St. Catherine and St. John the Baptist on one
side, and those of St. Francis and St.
Anthony of Padua on the other. It
also bears his inscription of "Antonio
de Allegris." It is painted on wood,
and the dimensions are 10 French feet
4 inches, by 8 feet 6 inches.

From the old records of a law-suit,

it appears that there was a picture of the Virgin and Child, with figures of other Saints, by Correggio, in the chapel belonging to the family of Invisiati, in the church of St. Nicholas, at Carpi; and Tiraboschi conjectures, from the dress of the figures, that the piece now preserved at Dresden, is this identical performance, because they are habited like the Friars belonging to that convent.[L] According to the opinion of Mengs, it is in the first style of Correggio, executed, in general, with great spirit and softness, though with a little harshness in the contours. "The colouring," he observes, "is true and rich, and in a style between that of Perugino and Leonardo da Vinci. The head of the Virgin," he adds, "greatly resembles those of da Vinci, particularly in the cheeks and in the smiling countenance. The folds of the drapery appear as if done by Mantegna, that is, in the mode of encircling the limbs, but they are less dry and more grand."

The next performance in order of time, appears to be the picture which is also preserved in the Gallery at Dresden, formerly called the St. Pietro Martire, and now known by the appellation of the St. George,[M] which was executed for the brethren of St. Peter the Martyr, at Modena. It represents the Virgin holding the Child in her lap, seated on a throne surmounted with an arch, supported by two golden figures of Cherubim. On the right, near the Virgin, is St. Peter the Martyr, in the attitude of intercession; on the left, St. Geminiano, taking from the shoulder of an Angel the Model of a Church, as if to present it to the infant Saviour, whose hands are eagerly stretched forth to receive it. In the front are the two figures of St. John the Baptist and St. George, whose attitudes are contrasted with singular skill. St. John, who is represented as in the flower of youth, is partly turned towards the front, and pointing to the infant Saviour, as if to solicit attention. He is drawn nearly naked; and the anatomy is not only well studied, but designed with the usual grace of Correggio. On the opposite side, St. George, who gives the appellation to the piece, is exhibited as half turned, and looking towards the spectator. He is bareheaded, but in armour, with the right foot trampling on the head of a dragon, and holding a lance in the left hand. His form combines manly dignity with graceful ease; and is so bold in the relief, that it appears to be starting from the canvas.

In the front, between these two striking figures, are four small Angels of peculiar beauty, and strongly contrasted in attitude. Two on the base of the throne are attempting to place the helmet of the Christian hero on the head of a third, and in front is the fourth, in the act of drawing his sword, with an air of infantine and fascinating playfulness." Guido, who is as well known for his acute and whimsical remarks, as for his professional merits, was so delighted with these exquisite figures, that he asked a friend who had recently returned from Modena, "Have the children of Correggio grown up and walked, or are they still to be found in the picture of St. Pietro Martire, where I last left them?"[x]

The picture is 10 French feet in height, and 6 feet 8 inches in breadth. It was placed as an altar-piece; and from the original design, formerly in the possession of M. Marietti, at Paris, the body of architecture in the painting was connected with a similar architectural decoration, delineated on the wall, which must have considerably heightened its effect.

This performance is highly valuable as a specimen of his second, or intermediate style;[M] for though it is far superior to the picture last mentioned, in the elegance of the contours, the harmony of the colouring, and the character and movements of the figures, it is yet comparatively inferior, in that general and magic effect of the clear obscure, which marks the productions of his best style. The colouring of the figure of St. George strongly resembles that of Giorgione.

We cannot doubt that Correggio was constantly employed at this period; but we have authentic documents to ascertain the date of only a single picture. This was an altarpiece for the church of Albinea, which is now lost, and of which the subject is unknown. The price is not ascertained; but a record remains, proving that the parishioners paid him thirty soldi a day for his maintenance, during the time of his work, and his final receipt is extant, dated 14th October, 1519, for the last payment of four gold ducats, in full of all demands.* It is also said, that this picture was removed from the church, by Alfonso, Duke of Modena, who replaced it with a copy by Boulanger, his painter, and forgave the community a debt due to the ducal chamber. We adduce this merely as another proof that Correggio was employed in painting for convents and churches, and therefore that his reputation was at this time established.

The successful traffic of his father, Pellegrino, and his own no less successful labours, essentially raised the property and respectability of the

---

* Pungileoni, t. ii. p. 109.

family. In 1492 and 1513, Pellegrino
had been appointed to present the
annual offering of the revenderoli, or
retailers, to the patron saint of the
city. But in 1518* he appears under
the more honourable distinction of
representative of the mercanti. In
consequence of this increasing pros-
perity, the father had now the satisfaction to see both his son and
daughter advantageously settled. In
June, 1519, Catharine, his only sur-
viving daughter, espoused Vincenzio
Mariani, of St. Martino, in Rio, and
conveyed to him a dowry of one hundred ducats.° Pellegrino even engaged with his new son-in-law in the
cultivation of a farm, situated in the
· Villa di Stioli, of which a lease for
nine years was granted to them by the

-----

* Pungileoni, t. ii. p. 277.

proprietor, Pietro de Scurtis, for the sum of one hundred and fifty ducats, payable within the space of a year, fifty being deposited in advance.[*]

In the month of July ensuing, Antonio espoused, in her seventeenth year, Girolama, daughter of Bartolomeo Merlini, formerly an esquire to the Marquis of Mantua, and who had honourably fallen at the battle of Taro, in November, 1503. Her dowry consisted of a moiety of certain houses, lands, and moveables, held in joint property with her uncle, Giovanni Merlini, for which she afterwards received the sum of two hundred and fifty-seven ducats.[†] In the marriage deed of settlement she is

[*] Pungileonl, L. li. p. 114.
[†] Ibid. p. 150—Tiraboschi, L. vi. p. 290.

distinguished by titles at that period
applied only to persons of birth and
condition.[p]   She is said to have been
a woman of great beauty, and is supposed by Pungileoni to have been
taken by her husband as the pattern
of the delightful picture called the
Madonna Zingarella, from the gipsey
costume exhibited in the head-dress
of the Virgin.

With these events of his life, we
shall connect three pictures on the
same subject, though probably not of
the same date, because one of them
is supposed to have owed its origin to
the nuptials of his sister.   The subject of these pictures is the Marriage
of St. Catherine.

The first is a small painting, formerly in the possession of Count Bruhl, prime minister to Augustus the Third, King of Poland and Elector of Saxony.   It bears the inscription, "Laus Deo. Per Donna Matilda d' Este. Antonio Lieto fece il presente quadro, per sua divozione, anno 1517." Although the authenticity of this inscription has been questioned, because there was no princess of Este of the name of Matilda living at this period, Mengs admits it to be an original, and declares the painting most beautiful. It is said to have been presented to Count Bruhl by the Duke of Modena, when his royal master purchased the collection. It descended to his son, and is now in the imperial Gallery of St Petersburgh.*

---

* Pungileoni, t. ii. p. 108.

The second belonged to the Farnese
Gallery at Parma, was conveyed to
Naples by Charles the Third, and
preserved in the collection of Capo
di Monte.   It is in size about 11
inches by 9.   The elegance and
beauty of this little piece have always
excited admiration.   It has accordingly been often copied by the best
painters, among whom we may reckon
Annibal Caracci, but still maintains
its character for inimitable excellence.
It exhibits a singular combination of
attitudes, united with the utmost
grace and simplicity.   The Virgin
and St. Catherine are painted in
profile, the one sitting, the other
kneeling.   The Saviour is exhibited
in front, as a boy of eight or nine
years, sitting on the lap of his mother,
one leg resting on the ground, and the

other partly foreshortened, and bearing in his countenance a peculiar expression of youthful curiosity and attention. But the singular art of the painter is manifested in the disposition of the six hands, which appear nearly to touch each other, yet without constraint or affectation; and the grace with which the Virgin directs the hand of the boy, in placing the ring on the finger of the bride, is truly admirable. The harmony of the piece and the disposition of the lights and shades, exhibit proofs of that excellence which characterizes the pencil of Correggio.[q]

Another picture on the same subject, with the addition of a figure of St. Sebastian, and a representation of his Martyrdom in the back ground, appears to have been painted by Correggio for his friend, Doctor Francesco Grillenzoni of Modena.[R] In the possession of that gentleman it was admired and copied by Girolamo Carpi, who visited Modena, to examine some of the works of Correggio, and who, by his communications to Vasari, has enabled us to authenticate this painting. It is supposed to be that now preserved in the Royal Gallery of France.

By the same authority we are enabled to ascertain the authenticity of another painting, which has been greatly admired. This is Christ appearing to Mary Magdalen in the Garden, which first awakened the admiration of Girolamo Carpi for the compositions of Correggio. It

was then in the possession of the
Ercolani family at Bologna, appears
afterwards to have passed into the
hands of Cardinal Aldobrandini, and
finally, being purchased by Don Ramiro
Nugnez, duke of Medina de las
Torres, was transferred to the grand
collection in the Escurial.[8]

At this period of his life we find
Correggio principally resident in his
native town, as his name occurs, at
different epochs, in several public
documents. Of these, one deserves
especial notice. In 1517 he received
from his maternal uncle, Francesco
Aromani, a donation of a house and
parcel of land, and the gift is described in the instrument, as a reward
for his merits and *pecuniary* assist-
ance, in the necessities of his uncle, as

well as a proof of the esteem in which
the donor held the qualities of his
mind and heart. This deed also furnishes evidence of the favour he enjoyed
with his sovereign; for it was executed
in the palace of Manfredo, and in his
presence, and sanctioned by his
authority. The donation, however,
did not take effect till after the death
of his uncle, and eventually exposed
him to a long and vexatious litigation
with the Aromani family, by whom
its validity was strongly contested.*

---

* Pungileoni, t. l. p. 88; t. ii. p. 127.

NOTES

TO

CHAPTER I

OF THE

LIFE OF CORREGGIO.

———

NOTE A . . . . : . *Correggio was born in 1493 or 1494.*

No evidence has been produced of the exact date of his birth or baptism; but many writers now coincide, in admitting the validity of the date inserted in the monumental inscription raised, at the beginning of the last century, to his memory, in the Church of the Franciscans, where his remains were interred. This in-

scription states him to have died in 1534, at
the age of 40, which would fix his birth about
the beginning of the year 1494. Clementi Ruta,
who made many researches into his history,
distinctly states that he died of a malignant fever,
in 1534, at the age of 40 years and 7 months,
which would carry his birth to September or
October, 1493. This opinion is in a great
degree corroborated by the engagements into
which he entered for his works. For, in the
agreement with the Convent of St. Francesco,
at Correggio, dated August 30th, 1514, he is
mentioned in terms which shew that he was
then in his minority, or under 25, " cum
consensu patris," &c.; and in that with the
Fabric Masters of the Cathedral of Parma,
dated March 3rd, 1522, no mention is made of
the consent of his father, but the contract is
drawn in his own name, which proves that he
had then attained his majority. Comparing
these two periods, it is obvious that there cannot be any material error in fixing his birth
in the latter end of 1493 or the beginning of
1494. These documents are printed in Pungileoni, t. ii. p. 67 and p. 183.

Pungileoni likewise refers to two autographic letters, still extant in his native town, which, he observes, seem to circumscribe his birth to the period between the 1st of February and the 14th of October, 1494.

We have thought it proper to lay these various suppositions before the reader, because, if they do not absolutely decide the point, they at least limit the chance of error to a few months.

NOTE B . . . . *Manfredo, Nicolo, and Gilberto.*

Nicolo died in 1508, and his son Galeazzo, who succeeded him in the joint sovereignty, in 1517, Gilberto in 1518, and Manfredo in 1546.

NOTE C . . . . . . *Veronica Gambara.*

This princess was one of the most accomplished and interesting women of the age. She was the daughter of Count Giovanni Francesco, of the noble family of Gambara, who took their title from a small village in the Bresciano. She was born at Prato Alboino, in the vicinity of Brescia, in 1485. From her earliest years she was devoted to the study of polite and scientific literature, and her talents were fostered and improved by the learned Cardinal Bembo, from whose instructions she derived that elegance of taste, which rendered her so celebrated. She espoused Gilberto, prince of Correggio, in 1508, and rendered his court the abode of letters and philosophy. Losing her husband in 1518, she divided her time between the cares of government, the study of letters, and the education of her two sons, Gilberto and Ippolito, then in their minority. She opened an academy, or literary society, in her palace, and encouraged, by her presence and example, the learned discussions of the eminent men, whom she drew to her court. In 1515 she paid a visit to Bologna, with her husband, Gilberto, and attracted the notice of Pope Leo X. and Francis the First, King of France, both judges of literary merit, by the last of whom she was warmly praised, as the most accomplished woman he had ever seen.

In 1530 she waited on the Emperor Charles
the Fifth at Bologna, of which city her brother
was governor. Her graces and talents so won his
favour, that he soon afterwards paid her a visit
at her own capital, which he repeated in
1532. Affection to her deceased husband induced her to refuse all matrimonial connexions,
though of the most honourable kind; and the
cultivated talents of her two sons, whose merit
raised them to the Roman purple, afford
ample proof of her maternal care.

She died on the 13th of June, 1550. Her
various acquirements are the theme of general
admiration among the Italian writers, and she
appears to have held a correspondence with the
most celebrated characters of her time, princes,
warriors, and men of letters. She wrote Latin
with purity and elegance, but the works from
which her literary reputation is derived, are in
her native language, and have been published
under the title of *Rime e Lettere di Veronica
Gambara*. This collection has passed through
several editions. Her prose is pure and elegant,
and her verse has been honoured by a comparison with the sonnets of Petrarch.

This account is principally drawn from the

Biblioteca Modenese of Tiraboschi, art. Veronica Gambara.

NOTE D . . . . . *Andrea Mantegna.*

Andrea da Mantegna was born of humble
parents, in the vicinity of Padua, in 1430,
and, at an early age, attracted the notice of
Squarcione, who had travelled into Greece, and
revived the study of the antique.   Under
him, who had recently established a school
of painting at Padua, Mantegna improved
himself in the knowledge of design, perspective,
and expression, and was treated by him with
all the tenderness and affection of a father.
Perceiving, however, that the style of Squarcione wanted that richness of colouring, which
began to distinguish the school of his rival,
Giacomo Bellini, who was settled at Venice,
Mantegna irrecoverably offended him, by at-
taching himself to that master.   In return, he
obtained the patronage of Bellini, espoused his
daughter, and was a fellow-pupil with his
brothers-in-law, Giovanni and Gentili Bellini,
the leaders of the Venetian school.

Uniting, in an eminent degree, the characteristics of Squarcione and Bellini, Mantegna became so celebrated, as to obtain the patronage of Ludovico Gonzaga, Marquis of Mantua. Removing, therefore, to that capital, he established the school of art, which illustrated the House of Gonzaga. He was next invited to Rome, by Pope Innocent the Eighth, and, though scantily rewarded for the labours of his pencil, he availed himself of his residence in that capital, to improve his knowledge of the antique, and to study the productions of those masters, who preceded Raphael and Michael Angelo.

After the death of Innocent, in 1492, he repaired to Florence, where new beauties were offered to his discerning eye, in the works of the Florentine masters, and in those of Fra. Bartolomeo and Leonardo da Vinci; and he returned to fix his permanent residence in Mantua, improved in the practice of his art, and enriched with an ample collection of models and copies, which he had made from antique statues and the works of the best painters. From his few productions which are still extant, we find that although he could not

entirely divest himself of the dry colouring of
Squarcione, he had imbibed that grace of
form, and beauty of countenance, which mark
the works of Leonardo da Vinci, whom he
seems to have imitated with peculiar zeal.

Mantegna is distinguished among the earliest
masters, after the revival of the art, for his skill
in fore-shortening, and in the clear obscure; and
that he was acquainted with both there seems
sufficient evidence. In the collection at Font-
hill Abbey is a picture from his pencil, the
subject of which is the Agony of Christ in the
Garden. The colouring is dry, and the disposition of the piece does not exhibit the skill of
later masters; but the figure of one of the disciples is fore-shortened in the boldest manner,
though there is not the slightest attempt to produce effect by means of the clear obscure. At
Hampton Court, however, another of his pictures is preserved, exhibiting the triumph of
Cæsar, in which the clear obscure is strikingly
introduced.

Mantegna died at Mantua, in 1506, and
was interred in the church of St. Andrea,
where a monument is erected to his memory,
surmounted with his statue in bronze.

It was long supposed that Mantegna lived till 1517, but Tiraboschi ascertained the period of his death, to be in 1506, from the original letters of his son.

Vasari — Abecedario Pittorico — Tiraboschi, Vita del Correggio, in the Biblioteca Modenese — Ticozzi, Dizionario de' Pittori, — and Lanzi.

Pungileoni asserts, on the authority of Antonioli, who had examined documents on the subject, that Antonio accompanied Manfredo, one of the joint sovereigns of Correggio, to Mantua, in 1511, while his native city was ravaged by the plague. He adds, that he was treated by that prince with great familiarity, and lodged in his palace. During this period he supposes that he studied the works of Andrea Mantegna, Leon Bruno, del Costa, and the elder Dosso, and derived advantage from the rich collection of cameos, medals, and antiquities, formed by the Princess Isabella d'Este. But he is inclined to doubt that he ever received instructions from Andrea himself, who had then been dead five years; and he denies that he could at this time have been taught by his sons, because Ludovico, the elder, was dead, and Francesco was living, in great distress, at Boscoldo. Of this visit, however, we find no positive proof; and even if it were admitted, it would in no way weaken the supposition, that Antonio had previously repaired to Mantua, while Andrea da Mantegna was living. Pungileoni, t. ii, p. 30, 31, 32.

Note E . . . . . *Francesco Bianchi.*

Francesco Bianchi Ferrari was a native of Modena, and flourished towards the latter end of the fifteenth century. He is honourably mentioned in the chronicles of the town, as having painted many pictures of considerable merit, and died on the 8th of February, 1510, without children, but possessed of considerable property, which he devoted to pious uses.

A passage has been generally quoted from the Chronicle of Lancillotto, a contemporary, which distinctly indicates him as master of Correggio, namely, " Francesco del Bianco, pittor famoso, fu maestro del divino coloritoro

Antonio da Correggio." But the authenticity of this passage is strongly contested by Tiraboschi, who states it to have been interpolated by the copyist, Spaccini. However, as Spaccini lived within a century of the time, and was himself a painter, we may reasonably suppose that he derived his intelligence from living witnesses or tradition; and that there is some foundation for the opinion that Correggio studied under Bianchi. As the death of Bianchi did not happen till 1510, Correggio was then not less than sixteen, and must have made essential progress in the art, since we find that he painted a picture of considerable merit before he concluded his 20th year. It is likewise asserted, by Vedriani, that, in the school of Bianchi, Correggio studied modelling, and formed an acquaintance with the eminent sculptor, Begarelli, who afterwards furnished him with models for the figures in the cupola of the cathedral at Parma. It is even further said, that he assisted Begarelli in the beautiful groupe of la Pietà, in the church of St. Margaret, of which the three best figures are ascribed to him; and the initials A A, found under the arm of one of them, when they were removed, on the suppression of the church, have supplied an additional argument for ascribing them to Correggio, as indicating his name Antonio Allegri. There is, however, an authority of greater weight, in the additions to Lancillotto's Chronicle, made by Spaccini, who mentions that, in 1531, these figures were removed from the portico before the church, and states distinctly that they were by the hand of Begarelli. Hence Pungileoni justly controverts the opinion which assigns them to Correggio.

This fact is also confirmed by Father Malazeppi, in his manuscript History of his Order, finished in 1580. Pungileoni, t. ii, p. 196-7 —Lanzi, t. iv, p. 67—Tiraboschi, Biblioteca Modenese, t. vi, p. 390, 591.

Note F . . . . . *Giambattista Lombardi.*

Professor at Bologna, in 1490. He enjoyed the favour of his sovereigns in a high degree, was left as one of the regency, when they quitted their capital to escape the infection of the plague in 1511, and was frequently employed in the capacity of envoy to Mantua. Pungileoni, t. i, p. 34.

He is supposed also to have presided over the literary meetings held in the palace of Veronica Gambara.

NOTE G . . . . . *convents and religious houses.*

Some have supposed that the earliest exercise of Correggio's talents was shewn in the decoration of apartments in a palace erected by Gilberto, prince of Correggio, in the suburbs of that city. This assertion, however, rests entirely on vague conjecture; for the palace has been long destroyed, and no evidence is preserved, to prove that such paintings ever existed.

NOTE H . . . . . . *an agreement.*

Antonius fil. Peregrini de Allegris ibi præsens, per se cum consensu ejus patris præ-

sentis et consensum dantis, promisit et solemn-
iter convenit Ven. Viro Fratri Hieronimo de
Cataneis * * * se facere et pingere Anconam
unam, valoris et existimationis ducatorum centum
et plus, detractis lignamine et factura dicti lig-
naminis dictæ Anconæ, quam etiam lignamina
dictus Custos et Sindici teneantur suis sump-
tibus facere seu fieri facere ; et hoc fecit dictus
Antonius, quia dictus Custos promisit et solvere
convenit dare et exbursare dicto Antonio * *
ducatos quinquaginta, completa ipsa Ancona,
et eum ipse Antonius ipsam Anconam valoris
ut supra pinxerit et compleverit.   Et eo quia
ut supra dictus Custos dedit et actualiter nu-
meravit Do. Antonio præsenti ad se trahenti in
pecunia numerata ducatos quinquaginta * * *
Quæ omnia promisit dictus Custos et Antonius
habere rata, insuper juraverunt dictus Custos
supra pectus suum et dictus Antonius tactis
Scripturis.   Actum in Burgo veteri terræ
Corrigiæ, et in camera cubiculari dicti Ser Antonii ad terrenum."—*Dated* 30 *August,* 1514.

Pungileoni, t. ii, p. 66.

NOTE I . . . . . *last prince of Correggio.*

After enjoying its independence as an Imperial fief, for several centuries, under its native sovereigns, Correggio, in the middle of the seventeenth century, was annexed to the dominions of the House of Modena. The plea for this transfer was, an accusation preferred against the last prince, Giovanni Siro, for the falsification of the coin. Being subjected to a fine of 230,000 florins, which he was unable to pay, his domain was occupied in 1633, by the Spanish court, as a pledge for that sum, which they advanced to the Imperial chamber. The dukes of Modena being desirous of appropriating a territory, which was situated in the midst of their dominions, obtained its transfer from Spain, on the condition of reimbursing the fine, and assisting the House of Austria in the war in which they were then engaged against the French and the Protestant powers. The possession was at first conditional, but in 1649 it was rendered permanent by an agreement with Maurizio, the son of Siro, who, for a certain compensation, relinquished his title to his paternal sovereignty. Muratori, Antichità Estensi, t. ii, p. 54.

NOTE K . . . . . *an Antonio Correggio appears as a witness.*

Tiraboschi, t. vi, p. 257. Pungilconi questions this fact, and urges that the signature was that of a military commander, who bore that appellation. The point, however, is of little consequence to the merits of the case ; because, whether he was or was not at Carpi in 1512, the existence of a picture, by his hand, in the Franciscan church in that town, at a later period, is clearly established.

NOTE L . . . . . *the friars belonging to that convent.*

Doubts have been entertained whether this picture was painted for the Franciscans at

Carpi or those at Correggio. Among other arguments, it has been urged, that the space above the altar in the chapel of the Invisiati, where it is said to have been placed, was too small for the reception of so large a piece. A phrase, however, in the documents of the lawsuit mentioned in the text, appears to designate it with sufficient distinctness, for it is described as the " Tavola con la Santa Madonna e il suo figlio ed altri Santi, di mano del Correggio."

But, in the absence of more explicit evidence, the question must be left in uncertainty. The real point for consideration is undoubted, namely, that it is one of the earliest performances of Correggio, which have come down to posterity, and that it is in his first and comparatively dry style. The curious reader, who is desirous of further information, is referred to Tiraboschi, p. 244, and Pungileoni, t. ii, p. 70.

NOTE M . . . . . *second, or intermediate style.*

Pungileoni controverts the opinion of Mengs that the St. George was painted before Correggio began his great works at Parma, and conjectures that it was executed in 1532. He founds his decision on a proof far from being conclusive, for it is nothing more than a vague passage in the Chronicle of Lancellotti, stating that the community of St. Pietro Martire, at Modena, in that year caused their school to be painted, " fecè pitturare la sua scuola," which he interprets to mean an oratory or chapel. To make no observation on the indistinctness of this passage, it may as well apply to any other painter as to Correggio, and cannot weigh against the judgment of Mengs, on the internal evidence of the picture itself. However beautiful the figures, it is evidently of an earlier period than when Correggio brought the science of clear obscure to such perfection. Pungileoni, t. i, p. 216.

NOTE N . . . . . *of St. Pietro Martire where I last left them.*

Scannelli, quoted by Ratti, p. 97, note, and Pungileoni, t. i, p. 219. Vasari, on the authority of Girolamo Carpi, confirms the account that this picture was painted for that convent at Modena, and was copied by him at no great distance of time from its execution.   T. iv. p. 412.

Note O . . . . . . *a dowry of one hundred ducats.*

An acknowledgment of the payment of this sum appears in the documents of Zanotti, notary public. It was dated 26 June, 1521, and executed in the villa of Gilberto, prince of Correggio.

Note P . . . . . . *persons of birth and condition.*

" Magister Antonius Allegris * * * acceperit in uxorem * * * *honestam* mulierem *dominam* Hieronymam, fil. q. Bartholomei Merlini."   Her dowry is stated to consist of " domos, terras, res, et jura rationesque et actiones spectantes." Pungileoni, t. ii. p. 150.

NOTE Q . . . . . *the pencil of Correggio.*

Two copies of the Marriage of St. Catherine are preserved in the collection of Sir Richard Hoare, Bart., at Stourhead. The first is a drawing of the same size, and the second an enlarged copy by Cavalucci, a painter of Rome.

———————————

NOTE R . . . . . *Doctor Francesco Grillenzoni,*
of Modena.

Vasari, Vita di Girolamo da Carpi, t. v. p. 312. This marriage of St. Catherine has been engraved by Picart in two different ways. In the first the St. Sebastian, and the representation of his martyrdom are introduced; and, in the second, the saint is changed into an angel, and the martyrdom omitted.

Note S . . . . . . *collection in the Escurial.*

Vasari, t. iii. p. 62, t. v. p. 311. We have here taken implicitly the authority of Vasari, which is unquestionable, because it is directly derived from Girolamo Carpi himself, whom he knew at Rome in 1550, and of whose early pursuits and studies he has given a minute and interesting account.

CHAP. II.

WE now reach that period of Correggio's life, in which he may be said to have established his reputation, and to have shone forth, as the founder of a new style of painting. From the fame of his works, he seems to have attracted considerable notice at Parma;[A] and as his aunt Oliva Aromani was a native of that city, he probably by her means became known to the illustrious house of Montini. By the Cavaliere Scipione, a member of that family, he is said to have been patronized and recommended to Giovanna Piacenza, Abbess of the Monastery of St. Paulo, a lady of great taste and munificence, who was desirous of enriching her establishment with choice specimens of art, and who had already employed the ablest artists of the city, in embellishing the church and monastery, particularly Araldi in decorating the choir. By this noble

lady he was engaged to paint the
sides and vault of an apartment, which
she had herself erected, with subjects
of classical antiquity, in fresco. Part
of the work has been obliterated,
but various figures and ornamental
decorations are still left, in high preservation. Among these are an elegant frieze, ornamented with drapery,
vases, and the heads of goats; Boys or
Cupids, sporting with animals, and
emblems of the Chase; a figure of Juno
suspended in the clouds by a chain,
with the anvils at her feet, as described by Homer;* the Graces, and
the three sister Fates ; a Vestal with
a Dove, the emblem of virginity; a

---

* See an account of this singular punishment in-
flicted on Juno by Jupiter, Il. *i*, l. 19; Pope's Trans-
lation, Il. xv. 23.

Satyr; a Priestess sacrificing; For-
tune standing on the Globe; and
over the chimney, Diana riding in a
triumphal car, drawn by hounds, and
evidently intended as the principal
figure.

Not only from records of some
antiquity, but from internal evidence,
these paintings are proved to owe
their existence to the pencil of Correggio; and they have been considered particularly valuable in the
history of art, as furnishing a proof
of the time at which he adopted his
last and best style; for, the foreshortening is singularly bold, the
clear obscure presents all the magic
of his pencil, and the beauty and
grace of the figures are inimitable.
The date of the work is fixed,

with every appearance of truth, about
the year 1519,* and it was therefore
the earliest of his productions at
Parma. This painting owes its celebrity to the diligence of father Affò,
who examined it minutely, and spared
no research into its history. It was
commemorated by Lanzi;† and Pungileoni has not only minutely described it, but given a sketch of the
various opinions as to its merits and
history.‡

He is also said to have soon afterwards decorated a small cupola for
the monks of St. John, with a representation of the Assumption of St.

* The chimney bears the date of 1514, probably
the period of its construction.

† T. iv. p. 47.——‡ T. i. p. 77, and t. ii. p. 118—
Servitor di Piazza, Dial. 3.,

Benedict ; but this work is now defaced.[*]

The admiration which these and
other different performances excited,
doubtless induced the monks of St.
John to engage him in ornamenting
the grand cupola, and other parts of
their church.   The original agreement
has not been discovered, but various
entries have been found in the books
of the convent, between 1519 and
1536, which prove, that for adorning
the cupola he received, as Tiraboschi
asserts, 272 gold ducats, and 200
more for other parts of the fabric.[*]
The last payment of 27 gold ducats
was made on the 23rd of January,
1524, and the acknowledgment of

* Pungileoni, t. II. p. 126.

the painter, under his own signature,
is still extant.

The subject is the Ascension of
Christ in glory, surrounded by the
twelve Apostles, seated on the
clouds; and in the lunettes the four
Evangelists, and four Doctors of the
church. The situation of the painting
presented difficulties which none but
so great an artist could have overcome; for the cupola has neither
skylight nor windows, and consequently the whole effect of the piece
must depend on the light reflected
from below. The figures of the Apostles are chiefly naked, gigantic, and
in a style of peculiar grandeur.

Besides the cupola, various parts
of the same church were adorned by

his hand. He decorated the tribune, which was afterwards demolished to enlarge the choir,* and was so highly esteemed, that Cesare Aretusi was employed by the monks to copy it for the new tribune. He painted also, in fresco, the two sides of the fifth chapel on the right hand, the first representing the Martyrdom of St. Placido and St. Flavia, and the second a dead Christ, with the Virgin Mary swooning at his feet. Of these paintings Mengs particularly admires the head of St. Placido, and the exquisite figure of the Magdalen in the last-mentioned picture.

The pleasure which the monks derived from his works, even in their

---

* A fragment of this painting is said to be still preserved in the Ducal Library at Parma.—Servitor di Piazza.

incipient state, and their satisfaction
with his conduct in general, is manifested by a remarkable document.
This is a letter or patent of confraternity, passed in the general assembly
of the order, held at Pratalea, in the
latter end of 1521 ; a privilege which
was eagerly sought at this and earlier
periods, and seldom conferred on persons not eminent for rank or talents.
It conveyed a participation in the
spiritual benefits derived from the
prayers, masses, alms, and other
pious works of the community, and
was coupled with an engagement to
perform the same offices for the repose of his soul, and the souls of his
family, as were performed for their
own members.*

* Tiraboschi, t. vi. p. 261.

During his stay at Parma, Correggio was engaged in other works. One of these is the Flight into Egypt, or the Madonna della Scodella, so called from a bason, which the Virgin holds in her hand. It was originally an altar-piece for a chapel in the church of St. Sepolcro, belonging to the Lateran Canons. According to the opinion of Mengs, the beauty of this picture was injured by a Spanish painter, who obtained permission to copy it; but Pungileoni asserts, that it still exhibits traces of the masterly hand, which produced the St. Jerome and the Notte."

The subject is a momentary repose of the holy family, during their flight into Egypt. The Virgin is seated under a palm tree, supporting the infant Jesus on one arm, and, with a bason in her right hand, taking water from a spring. Joseph appears arranging the branches of palm, as if to screen her from the heat, and at the same time gathering dates. Towards the edge of the picture, is an angel taking charge of the ass, which had borne the mother and child; and above flit a beautiful groupe of angels, surrounded with glory.[*] The author saw it remaining in its original situation in 1785.

Perhaps it may here appear not superfluous to advert to a painting ascribed to Correggio, less from its actual state of preservation, than from its history. It is a Madonna in fresco,

---

[*] Voyage d'un Amateur des Arts, t. iv. p. 49.

in the same grand style as the figures
in the cupola of St. John, supposed
to have been originally painted as a
decoration for the house of a friend in
Parma ; but it is said to have attracted
so much veneration, as to have become
an object of worship.   The house was
accordingly converted into a chapel,
the ascent to which is formed by
twelve steps, and has, consequently,
received the appellation of the Chapel
of the Madonna della Scala.   The
head of the Virgin has been surrounded, by some votary of wretched taste,
with a silver crown in relief.   The
colours are much faded, as if painted
in bistre ; but the design still exhibits
striking traces of the grace and grandeur of Correggio.*

---

* Voyage d'un Amateur des Arts, t. iv. p. 50.

While he was employed in this undertaking, Correggio fixed his residence in the Borgo Pescaro, near the church; but during the colder season, when he could not work in fresco, he appears to have returned to his native place. Passing through Reggio, in one of his journeys, he received a commission from Alberto Pratonero, which produced one of his finest pictures, The Nativity, or, as it is now called, La Nótte. The agreement was signed on the 14th of October, 1522, and the price fixed at two hundred and eight lire di Moneta Vecchia, which Tiraboschi* estimates at $47\frac{1}{2}$ gold ducats.

This picture is doubtless the most

* T. vi. p. 267.

singular, if not the most beautiful
work of this great master.   Adopt-
ing an idea hitherto unknown to
painters, he has created a new principle of light and shade; and in the
limited space of nine feet by six, has
expanded a breadth and depth of
perspective which defies description.
The time he has chosen, is the adoration of the shepherds, who, after
hearing the glad tidings of joy and
salvation, proclaimed by the heavenly
host, hastened to hail the new-born
King and Saviour.   On so unpro-
mising a subject as the birth of a
child, in so mean a place as a stable,
the painter has, however, thrown the
air of divinity itself.   The principal
light emanates from the body of the
infant, and illuminates the surrounding objects; but a secondary light is

borrowed from a groupe of angels
above, which, while it aids the general effect, is yet itself irradiated by
the glory breaking from the child, and
allegorising the expression of Scripture, that Christ was the true light of
the world.*   Nor is the art with which
the figures are represented, less admirable than the management of the
light.   The face of the child is skilfully hidden by its oblique position,
from the conviction, that the features
of a new-born infant are ill adapted to
please the eye; but that of the Virgin is warmly irradiated, and yet so
disposed, that in bending with maternal fondness over her offspring, it

---

* This groupe was particularly admired by Sir
Joshua Reynolds, and imitated by Rembrandt in
his picture of the Annunciation. ·

exhibits exquisite beauty, without
the harshness of deep shadows. The
light strikes boldly on the lower part
of her face, and is lost in a fainter
glow on the eyes, while the forehead
is thrown into shade. The figures of
Joseph and the shepherds are traced
with the same skilful pencil; and the
glow which illuminates the piece, is
heightened to the imagination, by the
attitude of a shepherdess, bringing an
offering of doves, who shades her
eyes with her hand, as if unable to
sustain the brightness of incarnate
Divinity. The glimmering of the
rising dawn, which shews the figures
in the back ground, contributes to
augment the splendor of the principal glory. "The beauty, grace,
and finish of the piece," says Mengs,
"are admirable, and every part is

executed in a peculiar and appropriate style."

It is uncertain when this picture was finished, for it was delayed by his other avocations, and he had long to struggle with the impatience of the Pratoneri for its completion.[*]   An inscription, still extant, proves, that it was not fixed in its destined place, the chapel of the Pratoneri, in the church of St. Prospero, at Reggio, till 1530. It was in 1640[B] removed surreptitiously, and probably by order of the reigning Dûke of Modena, who substituted a copy; and, with the pictures already described, it was finally transferred to the Electoral Gallery at Dresden.

---

[*] Pungileoni, t. ii. p. 196.

The St. Jerome, the second of these pieces, was painted for Briseis, a noble lady of Parma, the widow of Horatio or Octaviano Bergonzi. The commission was given in 1523,[F] and the stipulated price was four hundred lire, which Tiraboschi estimates at eighty golden crowns. We are informed likewise, that Correggio was lodged and maintained during the progress of the picture, and was besides gratified with occasional presents.

Of this celebrated painting, Annibal Carracci speaks in terms almost amounting to adoration, and his eulogy is fully corroborated by Mengs. After apologizing for the common anachronism of making St. Jerome contemporary with Christ, this artist critically investigates the merits of the piece. "It represents," he observes, " the blessed Virgin and Child, with St. Jerome in the act of offering his writings to the infant Jesus. Between the infant and the saint is an angel, pointing to some passage in the book. St. Jerome himself is represented with a violet drapery, carelessly thrown over his shoulders ; and the naked parts of the body are depicted with a perfect knowledge of anatomy, and the highest beauty of colouring. At his feet is his majestic emblem, the lion. On the opposite side is Mary Magdalen, bending to kiss the foot of Jesus, with a countenance expressive at once of respect, love, and adoration ; and nearly behind her, is an angel smelling to a vase, to indicate the offering made by her of the box of precious ointment, mentioned in Scripture. This picture merits a high place among the most beautiful paintings of Correggio, and may be justly compared with the small Magdalen and the celebrated Nôtte. It exhibits a body of colour unexampled in richness, and, at the same time, the almost incompatible quality of equal clearness. With this the tints are bright and varied, yet so intimately blended, that they appear infused into each other, like wax melted on the fire." Mengs adds, "Although the whole composition is wonderful, yet the head of the Magdalen is pre-eminent in beauty; and he who has not seen it, is ignorant of the effects which the pencil can produce."

This picture was given by the purchaser to the church of St. Antonio

Abbate, at Parma, in the year 1528.
One of the abbots having entered into
a treaty for its sale to the King of
Portugal, at a considerable price," the
community appealed to the Sovereign,
the infant Don Philip, by whose
order it was transferred to the cathedral.   In 1756 it was placed in the
Academy of Painting, which he had
then instituted.   Here the writer
of this narrative saw it in 1786,
and admired, not only its beauty, but
its wonderful freshness, for it appeared
as perfect as if just taken from the
easel. It was removed by the French,
in the plunder of Italy, and was one
of the most conspicuous ornaments of
the Louvre.   When the spoils of
nations were again wrested from
France, it was restored by the Allied

Powers to its original situation, and still attracts to Parma the admirers of Correggio, and the lovers of the fine arts.

It is here proper to advert to another picture of great celebrity, of which Pungileoni seems justly to fix the date about this period. This is the St. Sebastian, which was painted for the confraternity of St. Sebastian, at Modena; but not, as Mengs conjectures, in fulfilment of a vow, made when the city was visited by the pestilence.

The subject is the Virgin in glory, bearing in her arms the infant Jesus. She is surrounded with clouds, amidst which are flitting beautiful groupes

of cherubim and seraphim, and
below are the figures of St. Sebastian, St. Geminiano, and St. Roque.
.St. Sebastian, from whom the picture
takes its name, is represented as tied
to a tree, in a posture of supplication.
He is naked from the girdle upwards,
and furnishes a striking example of
the exquisite knowledge of the painter
in anatomy ; for while the countenance expresses ardour and hope, the
tense nerves, turgid veins, and swollen
muscles, convey the strongest indi-
cation of extreme, yet patient anguish.
The St. Geminiano appears listening
to one of the angels near the Virgin ;
while, at his feet, a young female, of
supernatural beauty, holds up, as if
to present to the infant Jesus, the
model of the church of Modena, of
which that saint is patron. St. Roque

is depicted behind, resting on a rugged
bed of rock, as if abandoned and in-
fected by the plague.

But the grace of the figures, however striking, is not the highest merit
of the picture; for the disposition
of the lights and shades, and the
surprising harmony of the whole,
have awakened the admiration of the
most profound judges. Mengs, in
particular, dwells with rapture on the
blaze of glory diffused over the piece,
which, though consisting only of a
bright yellow, is so admirably scat-
tered, and so skilfully contrasted with
the shadows, as to produce the full
effect of the sun-beams, without diminishing the spirit of the figures, or the
lustre of the tints. From this glow
of radiance, the Virgin and Child ap-

pear to emerge, as from an obscure
ground; and to give their figures the
full effect, the light is partially and
fancifully distributed on those below.

Mengs considered the St. Sebastian
as one of Correggio's best productions
before he was employed at Parma.
In this instance, however, he does
not seem to have manifested his usual
discernment; for the whole character
of the piece, and in particular the
management of the clear obscure,
seem to assign it to a more advanced
period, when the painter had attained
his last and best style. This opinion
is corroborated by historical evidence;
for, according to the Chronicle of Lancillotto, as quoted by Pungileoni,
the church of the community of St.
Sebastian was not rendered fit for

divine service till 1524; and it is not likely that the picture would have been ordered and painted, seven years before the church, for which it was designed, was ready for its reception. Here we find it soon after the death of Correggio; for it was one of the pictures copied by Girolamo Carpi, before the middle of the sixteenth century.*

The St. Sebastian was taken from the church by Alphonso, the fourth, Duke of Modena, who, as a compensation, gave the community a copy, and defrayed the expense of painting their choir by Colonna and Metelli. It passed, with the rest of the Modenese collection, to the Gallery of Dresden, where it is still preserved.

* Pungileoni, t. i. p. 154.—Vasari, t. v. p. 313.

Its dimensions are 9 French feet 7 inches, by 8 feet $6\frac{1}{2}$ inches.

The high credit which Correggio had derived from his various performances, procured him new commissions before he had finished the works in which he was engaged. Scarcely, therefore, had he commenced his operations in the church of St. John, when he was solicited to paint the cupola, and other parts of the cathedral. The contract ,which he signed on the 3rd of November, 1522, is preserved in the archives, and was lately published by his biographer, Pungileoni,[1] from a copy taken and authenticated by a notary public, in the year 1803.

In the estimate, or plan, which he drew up at the desire of the chapter, and which is still preserved in his own hand-writing, he required twelve hundred gold ducats, including one hundred for leaf-gold; the scaffolding, lime, and other requisites to be provided by the chapter; but in the contract itself this sum was reduced to one thousand, exclusive of the one hundred for leaf-gold. For this he engaged to paint the choir and cupola, with its arches and pillars, as far as the altar, exclusive of the lateral chapels, in imitation of living subjects, bronze, or marble, according to the plan prescribed, and in conformity to the nature of the place, comprising, in the whole, a surface of 154 square pertiche or perches.*

---

* The Italian pertica is equal to 17½ feet English in length.

The masters of the fabric were, on their part, to furnish one hundred ducats, in leaf-gold, for ornamenting the said painting, and to provide the scaffolding and lime, as well as to defray the expense of preparing the wall.[x]

The difficulties with which Correggio had to contend in the decoration of the cupola of the cathedral, were still greater than those in the church of St. John, and he has vanquished them with superior skill and felicity. This dome, which is nearly thirty-nine feet in diameter, is octagonal, the compartments diminishing as it rises; and it is not surmounted with a lantern, but towards the lower part enlightened by windows, approaching to an oval form. On this

surface he has delineated numerous
groupes of figures, with extraordinary
boldness and effect; though, for the
sake of variety, he has partially
adopted a smaller scale than in the
cupola of St. John. The subject is
the Assumption of the Virgin Mary.
She is represented with an air, in the
highest degree indicative of devotion
and beatitude, as rising to meet
Christ in the clouds, surrounded by
the heavenly choir of saints and
angels; while beneath, the apostles
behold her reception into glory with
the most dignified expression of
reverence and astonishment.   Over
the whole is an effusion of light,
which produces an impression truly
celestial.

The figures, which are depicted in

the upper part of the dome, are foreshortened with consummate skill. Mengs, who saw them near, and judged of them as an artist, appears astonished at their boldness, which he calls " sconcia terribile," particularly that of Christ, which occupies the centre. But the effect, when seen from below, proves that the painter had deeply studied this delicate branch of art; for nothing can exceed the bold and exquisite management of the light and shade, and the beautiful proportion in which the figures appear to the eye, except the life and spirit with which they are animated, and the general harmony of the whole.

In decorating the lower part of the cupola, Correggio has displayed undiminished resources. He has figured a species of socle, or cornice, which runs round the whole cupola, yet at such a distance as to afford a space between the windows for the Apostles, who appear, some single, some in pairs, surrounded with angels, and delineated in the same grand style as those in the cupola of St. John. Yet, although placed on the very lines of the angles, formed in the dome, they are so artfully disposed and foreshortened, as to appear painted vertically on the cornice. To unite these with the principal figures, he has distributed above, and on the socle, groupes of angels, some with torches, others bearing vases and censers, and of an intermediate size, between the gigantic figures of the Apostles, and the light and airy forms of the celestial choir above.

But a striking proof of his taste and skill is manifested in the four lunettes, between the arches supporting the cupola. Here he has feigned the architecture to form four capacious niches or shells, in which he has introduced the patrons of the city, St. John the Baptist, St. Hilary, St. Thomas, and St. Bernard degli Uberti, in magnitude equal to the Apostles, resting on clouds, and attended by angels. Depicting the light, as transmitted from the groupes above, he has so naturally thrown it upon these figures and their angelic suite, that they appear as if detached from the wall, and animated with more than human spirit and grace.

He has added various decorations, consisting of festoons of fruits and flowers, painted with no less truth than the figures, which produce the happiest effect, and give harmony and variety to the whole composition.

This performance is described by Mengs, as the most beautiful cupola ever painted, and by Ratti as a prodigy of art; and we shall hereafter find, that it called forth the warmest testimony of approbation from the Carracci, the founders of the Bolognese school. Mengs justly observes, that one of its peculiar excellencies consists in the number of figures, the grouping and disposition of which required such consummate science, fancy, and skill. So admirably indeed has Correggio adapted his performance to the place, that the architecture appears rather to have been planned for the painting, than the painting designed for the architecture.

In comparing this cupola with that of St. John, we are struck with the singular contrast which they present. In the latter, the figures, all bold and gigantic, evince the highest degree of sublimity and majesty ; while in the former, their variety, their number, and their disposition display the richest fancy, the finest taste, and the utmost fertility of invention, combined with the most perfect art. In fact, to the grandeur of his first conception, Correggio has here united an equal degree of beauty, elegance, and grace; and were it not for historical evidence, and the characteristic

traces of his pencil, we should be led
to consider these two wonderful performances as the works of two different masters.

In order to overcome the difficulties
which the peculiar shape and angles
of the dome presented, many of the
figures are supposed to have been
painted from models in chalk, said
to be formed by his friend Begarelli, whose skill as a statuary
received the praise even of Michael
Angelo. It is also a curious fact, that a
model of this kind was found towards
the close of the last century, on the
soffit of the cupola, by Giuliano Tra-
ballese, a Florentine painter, and di-
rector of the Royal Academy at Milan.[*]

* Ratti.

At all events, the sedulous attention
of the painter in the design and composition of this his greatest work, is
proved by the numerous sketches and
cartoons of various portions, which
are still extant in Italy.[L]

He seems to have commenced this
cupola as late as 1525, or 1526; for
on the 29th of November 1526, he
received the sum of seventy-six
gold ducats, as the last payment of
the first instalment of two hundred
and seventy-five ducats; and in 1530
an entry occurs in the private archives
of the chapter, recording the payment
of one hundred and seventy ducats,
as the last part of the second instalment, promised for this performance.[M]
No document, however, has been
found to prove the receipt of any

other payment, and the work appears
to have been prosecuted only at in-
tervals; as we observe that, during the
colder season, he removed to his
native city, and was frequently ab-
sent, in consequence of law-suits with
the family of his wife. His work was
also obstructed by his other engagements, and likewise by the feuds and
warfare, which at this period agitated
Parma, and the neighbouring parts of
Lombardy. It has even been supposed, and not without foundation,
that some dispute arose between him
and the canons of the cathedral, who
are said to have disgusted him by their
tasteless interference. An anecdote
has been related, that while he was
employed in the work, they were so
dissatisfied with the smallness of
many of the figures,[N] that they ap-

pealed to Titian, who visited Parma in the suite of the Emperor Charles the Fifth, for his opinion, whether they should cancel the whole, or suffer the painter to proceed; and that they were diverted from their purpose by the reply of Titian, that it was the finest composition he had ever seen. But whatever may be the truth or falsehood of this anecdote, if we may rely on an expression of Bernardino Gatti, one of his scholars, he had conceived some deep chagrin from the conduct of his employers; for Gatti being engaged to paint the chapel of the Steccata, made many objections, and required many securities, assigning as a reason, that he was unwilling to remain at the discretion of so many masters, and adding to his friend, " Remember what was said

to Correggio respecting the cathedral."*

His latest biographer, Pungileoni,
has indeed proved, that so far from
having completed his original undertaking, he left even a part of the
cupola itself unfinished; for he has
adduced documents, shewing that the
completion of the task was first assigned to Georgio Gandini,° one of his
scholars, and after his death, in 1538,
to Girolamo Bedoli, surnamed Mazzola.   The contract with this painter
evidently implies that some dissatis-
faction had been conceived against
Correggio by his employers, on a point
which evinces their inability to estimate the merits of his pencil; for a

---

* This letter of Gatti, containing this remark, is
quoted in the Servitor di Piazza.

part of the engagement consisted in a stipulation, that Bedoli should remove the gilding laid on the cupola by Correggio, which is said to have been of inferior metal, and replace it with pure leaf-gold, employing oil size[q] as the medium of adhesion.   Another memorandum, preserved in the books of the chapter, contributes to throw some light on the close of the transaction ; for in the register stating the expenses from 1549 to 1550, we find an entry, that the heirs of Antonio, the painter of Correggio, were indebted to the establishment in the sum of one hundred and forty lire, which he had received in advance before he died, and left his work incomplete.[*]

Acute observers have also succeeded in discriminating the boundary of Correggio's labours; for it appears that he intended to delineate ten figures of children round the socle, but finished only six. The remaining four, which are under the arch leading into the capella maggiore, or choir, with the accompanying ornaments, were added by Bedoli, and their execution is so inferior, that it serves only to manifest the unrivalled superiority of the original designer.[*]

During the suspension of his works at the cathedral, Correggio received a commission, which indicates the high reputation he then enjoyed in Lombardy.

---

[*] Pungileoni, t. iii. p. 7.

Frederic, the second Duke of Mantua, desirous of presenting the Emperor Charles the Fifth with two excellent pictures, selected Correggio to paint them.[a] The subjects, according to Vasari, were Leda and Venus; but according to Mengs and Ratti, with more probability, Leda and Danaë. They were said to be so well executed, that Julio Romano, who was at the court of Mantua, declared he never saw such excellent colouring. A curious anecdote is recorded of their subsequent fate. Being sent by the Emperor to Prague, they were afterwards taken by the Swedes at the sack of that city, and conveyed to Stockholm, by order of Gustavus Adolphus. On his death, being neglected, they were discovered in the reign of Christina, degraded to the

purpose of window-shutters in a
stable, by Bourdon, a French painter,
whom she patronized. They were
repaired by her order, conveyed to
Rome, and after her decease, came
into the possession of Don Livio
Odescalchi, Duke of Bracciano,* by
whose heirs they were sold to the
Regent, Duke of Orleans; but by
the order of his son, who was shocked
at the nudity of the figures, the pictures were cut in pieces. A similar
fate, according to Mengs, happened
to the Io, ascribed also to Correggio,
which was in the same collection,
and probably obtained in the same
manner from the heirs of the Duke
of Bracciano; for the Duke of Or-

---

* Don Livio Odescalchi was related to Cardinal
Azzolino, who was the legatee of Christina.

leans himself cut out the head, and
burnt it. Coypel, a French painter,
afterwards collected the remnants of
the piece which were not destroyed,
and to which a new head was added
by another artist; and the picture
sold to the King of Prussia for a great
price, and placed in the Gallery of
Sans Souci. A Danaë, supposed to be
painted by Correggio, was preserved in
the Orleans collection, as acquired
from the heirs of Christina. It was
purchased by Mr. Hope, and is now
said to be at Paris.

Before the close of 1532, Correggio
resided in his native city, and we find
him mentioned in a document in De-
cember that year, a few days before
the second visit of Charles the Fifth
to that place. Soon after the de-

partute of the august monarch, he
was also engaged in a proceeding indicative of the high estimation in
which he was held by his sovereigns;
for he appears as a witness to the deed
by which Manfredo, prince of Correggio, constituted as his procurator
Paulo Brunorio, to receive from the
Emperor the investiture of his fiefs.
Whether he was presented on this
occasion to the Emperor is now uncertain; but the commission which
he had previously received from the
Duke of Mantua, and the favour of
his own sovereigns, would suggest
the inference, that he was not unno-
ticed by the head of the empire. At
all events, he still continued his residence at Correggio, where he was
probably employed in painting his
later works; for the recurrence of his

name as a witness, in several public documents, proves that he was there in January 1533, and subsequently to September the same year. In the ensuing January we find another proof of the favour of his sovereigns; for on the marriage of Ippolito, son of Gilberto, by Veronica Gambara, to Chiara da Correggio, daughter of Gian Francesco, he was selected as one of the witnesses to the marriage deed, by which the bride received a dowry of twenty thousand gold crowns.[*]

The last document extant relative to his labours, proves, that he was not unoccupied in his profession; for, in the beginning of 1534, he received a commission from Alberto Panciroli,

---

[*] Pungileoni, L. i. p. 247.

father of the celebrated Guido, to paint an altar-piece. The price and subject are not known, but he received in advance twenty-five golden crowns. Before, however, he could enter on the execution of his performance, he was seized with a malignant fever,[*] and died suddenly at Correggio, on the 5th of March, 1534, in the 41st year of his age. On the next day, he was buried in the family sepulchre, in the Franciscan convent of Minor Friars, and the following is the brief and simple record of a loss so fatal to the arts :

" Ai dì 6 di Marzo morì Maestro Antonio Allegri, depintore, e fu sepolto a 6 detto, in Francesco, sotto il portico."[†]

In the sexton's book we also find

---

[*] Ratti, p. 125.   [†] Ibid. p. 126.

an entry relative to the fees paid for
his funeral, and the services afterwards
performed for the repose of his soul.[a]
The fulfilment of the engagement with
Alberto Panciroli being thus prevented by his death, his father, on
the 15th of the following June, re-
paid to Paulo Burani, the agent of
Alberto, the twenty-five crowns which
he had received in advance; and the
acquittance, which is still extant,
alludes to the fact of his sudden and
untimely decease.[a]

We have already stated, that Antonio Allegri espoused Girolama, of
the family of the Merlini. Some
authors, however, have involved even
this incident of his life in doubt, by

---

[a] Pungileoni, t. ii. p. 252.

giving him two wives, Girolama and Jacobina, the last from a palpable mistake in the baptismal record of his third daughter, in 1527, in which his wife is called Jacobina. The falsity of this inference is, however, fully proved, by a document, which shews his wife, Girolama, to have been living on the 22nd of March, 1528; for her father-in-law, Pellegrino, is then said to have acted in her name, and on her behalf.[a]

Pungileoni is of opinion, that she died soon after this period; but his supposition appears to rest on proofs too vague for a positive conclusion. These are, a passage in the will of Pel-

---

* Nomine et vice Hieronimæ, uxoris ejus filii, &c. Pungileoni, t. ii. p. 227.

legrino, executed in 1542, in which
she is mentioned as dead; and the
absence of any record relative to her
sepulture in the church of St. Francesco at Correggio, where she direct-
ed her body to be buried, in a testamentary disposition, made before her
marriage. From such data, and from
the silence of every subsequent record respecting her, he infers that she
did not die while she resided with her
husband at Correggio, and therefore
that her life must have terminated
during his stay at Parma, while he
was engaged in painting the cupola
of the cathedral.

It would, however, be of little im-
portance to ascertain the period of
her death, had not that event been
adduced as one of the causes which

prevented him from completing his
labours at Parma, by the affliction in
which he was involved, in consequence of such a loss.   But we
must leave this fact still in
doubt for want of evidence sufficiently decisive, and can only conclude, with certainty, that she did not
survive her father-in-law, who died
in 1545.

By his wife, Girolama, Antonio had
a son named Pomponio, who survived him.   She bore him also three
daughters, during the time he was
employed in painting the two cupolas
at Parma; for their births and baptisms
are recorded in the register of the convent of St. John.[T]

Two   of   these   daughters   died

young; but the eldest, Francesca, in 1546, espoused Pompeo Brunorio, and received from her paternal grandfather a legacy of no less than two hundred and fifty gold ducats.[u]

In this narrative we have hitherto confined our remarks to those paintings which, from authentic documents, are undoubtedly the productions of Correggio. Of his other works many still exist; and though they cannot historically be traced to his hand, yet their peculiar characteristics have induced the ablest judges to pronounce them his compositions. Of these, only four will be noticed, which, from the superior excellence of the clear obscure, manifest his pencil.

The subject of the first is the Agony of Christ in the garden. Our Saviour is represented in the act of prayer, with an angel in the air, pointing with one hand to the cross and crown of thorns, which are partly lost in shade, and partly irradiated in the foreground, and the other elevated, as if indicating the will of his Father, that he should be the propitiatory sacrifice for the sins of the world. Both these figures are boldly fore-shortened, particularly that of the angel, which appears to float in air. The expression is of the highest and most affecting character. The sorrow depicted on the face of the angel, though in profile, is unparalleled, and strikingly contrasted with the dignified resignation manifested in the countenance of the Saviour. The execution is excellent, but the management of the clear obscure peculiar to Cor-reggio. The light seems to descend from Heaven, and is reflected from the body of Christ on that of the angel. In the distance appear three of the disciples, and beyond are the officers and soldiers with the crowd. In this picture, as in the Nótte, the most refined skill is manifested in the representation of the distances, and the gradations of the lights ; and this beauty is here more striking, because so powerful an effect is produced on a scale extremely limited. At the first glance, only the figures of Christ and the angel are seen, illuminated with the glow of æthereal light ; and the rest of the picture appears enve-loped in nocturnal shade. On a closer examination, however, the other figures seem to emerge, and, as the eye dwells on the painting, the outline of the trees, the foliage, and the minuter details of the fore-ground, become gradually visible; thus exhibiting the true and almost inimitable effect of nature.[x]   On the whole, this picture, for harmony, brilliancy, and expression, is a matchless production.[*]   Its dimensions are 1 foot 4 inches and $\frac{3}{4}$, by 1 foot 3 inches and $\frac{1}{2}$.

Tradition absurdly states, that this gem was given by the painter to his apothecary, in discharge of a paltry debt of four crowns, and soon afterwards sold to one of the Visconti

---

* A beautiful and faithful copy of this exquisite picture has been made by John Jackson, Esq. R. A.

family for five hundred. All that we know of its history is, that it was purchased for Philip the Fourth, of Spain, by the governor of Milan, at the price of seven hundred and fifty Spanish doubloons, or 1,500*l.* sterling, and transferred to the palace of Madrid. It remained there till the invasion of Spain by the French, and on their retreat, was purloined by Joseph Buonaparte, and concealed, with other paintings, in the imperial of his carriage, in his flight from Madrid. It was, however, taken by the troops of our victorious army, and now graces the collection of the Duke of Wellington.

The second of these small but exquisite pieces, is the Penitent Magdalen, esteemed by many as the most fascinating of all his works. For whom, or at what period it was painted, is unknown, though the extreme care with which it is finished, proves that it was executed for some person of consequence, and probably towards the latter part of his life, when he had carried the clear obscure to the highest perfection.* From the earliest accounts extant, it was originally in the possession of the Dukes of Modena, and was considered as such an inestimable treasure, that whenever they quitted their capital, they conveyed it with them in a species of case, purposely formed in their carriage. It was no less highly prized by Augustus the Third, King of Po-

* Pungileoni conjectures that this Magdalen was painted by Correggio for the princes of Correggio, in order to be presented to the Emperor.

land and Elector of Saxony, who purchased it at the price of twenty-seven thousand Roman crowns, mounted it in a silver frame, adorned it with precious stones, and always kept it locked up in a case in his private apartment. After his death, being transferred to the Picture Gallery of Dresden, it was stolen a few years ago, by an unknown hand, but recovered by the offer of a great reward

The piece is painted on copper, and in dimensions does not exceed 20 inches by 15. The Magdalen is represented in a grotto, reposing on the ground, leaning on one arm, and perusing the Holy Scriptures, which rest on the other. The whole is thrown into shade, except the book,

the upper parts of the figure, and
the feet, which are naked. The
arrangement of the light is peculiar,
yet interesting, and admirably calcu-
lated to attract the attention to the
distinctive beauties of the female form;
for it falls in an oblique direction, and
is reflected from the sacred volume on
the arms, bosom, and countenance.
Over the shoulders is thrown a dark
blue drapery, which pleasingly contrasts with the carmine tints of the flesh.
A slight gleam of light is again caught
on the feet, which are naked and fore-
shortened, and within the dark part
of the picture; and it is gradually lost
in the back ground, which exhibits a
deep yet warm tint, subordinate to
that of the blue drapery. The
countenance is lovely, and the expression placid and intelligent. The

head is characterized by extreme simplicity, and the beauty of the hair is a
subject of general admiration, not
only from the softness of the colouring,
but from its lustre and delicacy, appearing, to use the expression of
Mengs, " as if each hair was painted
singly."

Another subject seems to have employed the pencil of Correggio, and
its execution is praised unequivocally
by the ablest judges. It is called the
Education of Cupid, and represents
Mercury teaching the infant deity to
read, in the presence of Venus. The
goddess of beauty is depicted with
ineffable grace. The Cupid exhibits
all the innocence of his age; his hair
is exquisitely finished, and his wings,
which are placed behind the shoul-

ders, so beautifully touched and so naturally adjusted, as perfectly to reconcile the eye to this fiction of painting. The Mercury displays all the flower of youth. A duplicate of this piece exists. That which Mengs considers as the original, was purchased by the Duke of Alva, from the collection of Charles the First, King of England, and was preserved in 1793 in the palace belonging to that family at Madrid.* The other, which is also admitted to be by the pencil of Correggio, first belonged to the Odescalchi family, was afterwards transferred to the Gallery of the Duke of Orleans, and, at present, we believe, is to be found in the collection at Sans Souci.

---

* Pungileoni, t. iii. p. 145.

Nor can we finally omit to notice the enchanting picture of Venus rising from the Sea, supported on the shoulders of two Tritons. A lover of the arts, who appears to have examined it with a discerning eye, dwells with rapture on the exquisite form of the goddess, the beauty and seducing air of her countenance, and the truth and brilliancy of the tints. He speaks with equal delight of the expression of astonishment and admiration manifested by the two Tritons.* It was in 1777 or 1778 in the possession of M. Bayer, an eminent antiquary and architect at Rome.

Other pieces are mentioned in various collections, with various claims

* Voyage d'un Amateur des Arts, t. iv, p. 44.

to authenticity. Of some of these, different duplicates or copies exist; others have been much damaged, or altered, and even partly effaced. On the merits or originality of these, we shall not presume to decide, but refer the curious reader to the catalogues given by Mengs, Ratti, Tiraboschi, and Pungileoni, the object of this sketch being chiefly to elucidate the few events of Correggio's life, to reconcile discordant opinions, and to record the history of those works which indisputably emanated from his hand.*

* Various authors have endeavoured to compile specific catalogues of the works of Correggio, but have failed in the attempt; and Pungileoni, his latest biographer, after enumerating the pieces ascribed to his pencil in different countries, in a list which fills fifty pages, concludes with acknowledging that it is impossible to ascertain the authenticity of many of these pictures.—Pungileoni, t. lil. p. 129 to 170.

NOTES TO CHAP. II.

NOTE A ...... *to have attracted notice at*
Parma.

A few remarks are here necessary, to shew
the situation of Parma during the time that
Correggio was employed in the works which
illustrate that city.

Like many other places of Italy, Parma,
with its appendage, Placentia, had been the
subject of perpetual struggles and feuds; sometimes independent, and sometimes ruled by the
neighbouring princes, among whom we may
enumerate those of Correggio. It subsequently
fell under the dominion of the dukes of
Milan, of the family of Sforza, in whose
possession it remained till the irruption of
the French into Italy. During the calamities
to which the House of Sforza were exposed,
it was ceded, in 1513, to Pope Julius the
Second. But, on the invasion of Italy by

Francis the First, it was transferred to him, in
1515, by Pope Leo the Tenth.   In 1521,
after the disasters of the French arms, it returned to the dominion of the Holy See, and,
notwithstanding the commotions which then
desolated Italy, it continued a domain of the
church till 1534, when it was erected into a
duchy by Pope Paul the Third, and conferred
on his natural son, Peter Louis, the founder of
the Farnese dynasty.

NOTE B ...... *the nave, and other parts of the*
fabric.

Much confusion prevails relative to the price
which Correggio received from the monks of
St. John, for decorating the cupola and
other parts of the church. This has arisen
from the diversity of the payments, which were
made at different times and by different persons,
and consequently entered in different books.
Father Affò, who examined the registers of
the monastery, stated the whole of the payments to Correggio, for the cupola, between 1521
and 1524, to have amounted to 272 gold

ducats ; and at the same time he published the
final receipt of Correggio for 27 ducats, dated
23 Jan. 1524. Vita del Parmegianino, p. 22,
note. The author of a Guide to Parma, under
the whimsical title of Servitor di Piazza,
quotes the whole amount of these payments,
from the Ledger No. 4, comprising the period
between 1519 and 1523, at 272 gold ducats,
for the different decorations in every part of
the church. Pungileoni, with his usual
accuracy, cites three several statements, from
as many books, which, though varying in the
items, make the same total of 272 gold ducats.
But father Zapata, as quoted by Tiraboschi,
after examining the registers, as well as a
cash-book now lost, comprising the period
between 1524 and 1536, distinctly states the
various payments made to Correggio for all his
labours in the said church at 472 gold ducats.
Tiraboschi, t. vi, p. 259, 260. To this account, as derived from a book, later in regard to
date, and consequently more accurate and com-
prehensive in its details, we are inclined to give
our full assent, more particularly, as it was
lost before the researches of Affò and Pungileoni.

NOTE C ...... *the Virgin Mary swooning at his feet.*

It has been generally supposed that Annibal Carracci copied this tribune ; but Pungileoni has proved that the copy was made by Aretusi.

NOTE D ...... *the St. Jerome.*

Bygge, in his Travels in the French Republic, asserts that, for this picture, Augustus the Third, King of Poland, and Elector of Saxony, offered 20,000 zecchines.

NOTE E ...... *It was in 1640 removed surreptitiously.*

Extract from a document belonging to the church of St. Prospero.

" Kal. Maj. à partù Virginia, 1640.

Tabula Jesu Christi natalia representans,

opus clarissimi pictoris Antonii à Corriggio,
ab ecclesiâ S. Prosperi noctu ablata * * *
omnibus civibus maximum dolorem attulit.
Pungileoni, t. ii. 212.

NOTE F ...... *the commission was given in 1523.*

Pungileoni mentions a sketch or first design
of this picture on oiled paper, which he considers
as by the hand of Correggio, dated January,
1524: it was in the possession of Signor Francesco Maria Trezzi, of Parma, who purchased
it in 1792.   Pungileoni, t. ii, p. 190.

NOTE G ...... *gratified with occasional presents.*

If we compare the prices paid for the St. Jerome and the Nótte, even with that of his earliest
work, which was 100 ducats, they seem dispro-
portionately small, particularly when we consider

that he was now in the height of his reputation, and liberally paid for the decoration of the churches at Parma. We must, therefore, suppose that he was remunerated in some other shape, particularly in provisions of various kinds; and that he was besides provided with the materials for executing the painting. This custom appears to have been common, as we find from many instances in the lives of other painters.

NOTE H .... *for its sale to the King of Portugal at a considerable price.*

Bygge, mentions that this offer was made in 1749, and that the price tendered was 40,000 zecchines.

NOTE I ......, *published by his biographer, Pungileoni.*

Copy of the agreement made with the Fabric

Masters of the cathedral for painting the cupola and other parts of the church :—

" Gratis undequaque inserviens Excellentissimo Serenissimo Domino Comiti Domino Bertioli Præsidi meritissimo supremi consilii justitiæ et patriæ Parmæ et Vastallæ.

" Reperitur in filsâ Rogitorum originalium contractuum receptorum ad quondam Dominum Stephanum Dodi, alias Notarium publicum Parmensem, existentem in hocce archivio publico Parmæ, inter cætera, adesse instrumentum tenoris sequentis, videlicet :

" Milesimo quingentesimo vigesimo secundo, Indictione decimâ, die tertiâ mensis Novembris. Reverendi Dominus Pasculius de Baliardis, et Galeaz de Garimbertis o Ambo Canonici Ecclesiæ Parmenais, Dominus Magnificus, Eques Auratus Dominus, Scipio dalla Rosa, Parmensis ; omnes Fabricantes Ecclesiæ prædictæ Parmensis et quilibet ipsorum tenoris præsentis publici instrumenti et omni meliore modo, sic jure et causa quibus magis et melius potuerunt et possunt dicto nomine et nomine vice fabricæ prædictæ Parmensis ecclesiæ sese convenerunt et conventionem fecerunt et faciunt cum magistro Antonio de Corriggio pictore, præsente,

conducente, stipulante, et recipiente pro se suisque hæredibus et successoribus, laborarium picturæ ecclesiæ prædictæ, hoe modo, et cum pactis,
modis, et conditionibus infrascriptis, videlicet :

" Primo che detto Maestro Antonio sia obbligato, quanto tiene il choro, la cupola co' suoi
archi et pilli, senza le capelle laterali, et directo
andando al sacramento, fassa, crosera, et nicchie
con le sponde, et ciò che di muro si vede su la
capella infino al pavimento, et trovatolo circa
a 150 pertiche quadre, da ornare de pitture con
quelle istorie vi saranno date, che imitano il
vivo, o il bronzo, o il marmo, secondo richiede
a li suoi lochi et il dovere della fabrica, et a
ragione e vagghezza de ipsa pictura a sue spese.

" Item che predicti Domini Fabricanti siano
obbligati et così promettono a dicto maestro Antonio, ducati cento in foglio per ornar dicte
picture et opera, et per la mercede sua de dicta
pictura, ducati mille de oro, et de dargli ponti
facti et la calcina da insmaltare, et le mure infalbato a la spese de dicta fabrica. Ex prædicta omnia effectura extendantur in forma cum
juramento et clausulis consuetis, de stilo mei
notarii infrascripti, et hæc omnia in præsentia
reverendorum

" Domini Jacobi de Colla,

" Domini Floriani Zampironi,

" Domini Latantii de Lalluta,

" Domini Eustachii de Ruore,

" Domini Jois Marci de Carissimis,

" Domini Latini de Baliardis,

" Domini Stephani Dena,

" Domini Jois Francisci de la Rosa,

" Domini Antonii de Rianis,

" Domini Camilli de Rianis,

" Domini Palencii de Garimbertis,

" Domini Ugolini de Lusébris.

" Omnium canonicorum dictæ ecclesiæ Parmensis, prædictis omnibus consentientium, &c.

" Peritia quæ adest inserta in hoc conventionum instrumento, est tenoris sequentis, scilicet . . .

" Visto diligente il lavoro che per ora val con vostre signorie, mi pare, piacendo a quello di patuire, che a pigliando quanto tiene il coro, la cupola con suoi archi e pilli, senza le capelle laterali et dintro andando al sacramento, fassa crosera e nicchie, con le sponde et ciò che di muro si vede, in la capella infino al pavimento, et trovatolo circa a 150 pertiche quadre da ornar di pittura, con quelle istorie mi sara dicta

che imitano o il vivo o il bronzo o il marmo,
secondo richiedo ai suoi lochi e il dovere della
fabbrica, et le ragioni e vaghezza da essa pictura,
e ciò a mie spese de 100 ducati de oro in foglio
et de colori et de calcina smaltade, che sarà
quello dove io pingerò sopra, non si potrà con
l'onore del loco e nostro fare per manco de
ducati 1200 de oro, et con il commodo de queste
cose

" 1. Prima dei ponti,

" 2. De la inserbadura,

" 3. De la calcina da smaltare, oltre a lo in-
serbare.

" 4. De un camerone o capella chiusa per
far li disegni.

" Actum Parmæ in ecclesiâ Parmensi præ-
sentibus ibidem venerabili Domino Patro de
Tebaldis, Domino Sebastiano de Belletis pres-
biteris Parmensibus et Laurentio de Palma
clerico Parmensi testibus ómnibus notis.

" Subscriptus—Rogatus per me Stephauum
Dodum Notarium. Ita ut supra reperiri at-
testor ego notarius archivista infrascriptus
ideoque hic pro fide me subscripsi, solitoque ar-
chivii prædicti sigillo muniri hac die 12 Florilis
anni XI Reipublicæ Gallicæ (2 Maj. 1803).

F. C. Carolus Callegari, Arch. Pungileoni,
t. ii, p. 182.

____

NOTE K .... *the expense of repairing the
wall.*

This appears to have been done by an agreement with Toria dell' Erba, mason, who, for the
sum of 200 imperial lire, engaged to remove
the former plastering of the cupola, and to lay
the ground of new stucco.

____

NOTE L ...... *still extant in Italy.*

Mr. Ford, of Gloucester Place, possesses a
sketch which he purchased at Naples, and
which is said to be an original design by this
inimitable master, for the dome of the cathedral;
it bears an inscription at the back A N. A L.
PINXIT IN MODENA, 1522, which is the very
year that the contract was signed with the
Masters of the Fabric, and in which he con-

cluded the agreement at Reggio for the Nótte. It is painted on thin cotton canvas, and is of an octangular form, to correspond with the shape of the dome. The groupes of figures and the distribution of the light appear, in general, similar to the painting of the dome; but in particular parts are important variations, which strongly indicate this sketch to be an original and preparatory design: for instance, the representation of the Almighty is introduced in the sketch, but not in the painting; and the Christ, who is represented as an adult on the dome, appears in the sketch as an infant on the bosom of his mother.

The sketch is stated to have been originally purchased at Modena, where it was executed, and to have remained, in the possession of the same family at Naples, upwards of seventy years.

From Mr. Ford's printed description of this curious production.

NOTE M ...... *second instalment promised for this performance.*

In Ratti, p. 72, the precise terms of the entry are thus given—" Pro resto secundi termini sibi promisi, pro pictura per eum facienda in ecclesia majori."

NOTE N ...... *dissatisfied with the smallness of the figures.*

Some have related, that one of the canons, in reference to the smallness of some of the figures, complained that Correggio had painted a fricassee of frogs (*guazzetto di rane*) ; others, that this contemptuous remark was made by one of the workmen. Lanzi.

Note O ...... *the task was first assigned to Georgio Gandini.*

The contract with Gandini is extant, and given by the indefatigable biographer of Correggio. It serves more fully to shew the portion of the engagement which he failed to complete; for Gandini was bound to ornament the capella maggiore or choir, the tribune or altar-end, and the faces of the two lateral chapels, together with the pillars. The subjects given, were an ornamented cross in mosaic, on a field of gold, on the vault of the choir. On the four sides of this cross, the figures of the saints, whose bodies are deposited in the cathedral, and other churches of the city. In the clouds, a field of pure azure. The façades of the two lateral chapels to be also ornamented with painting. On the right, the mission of the Holy Ghost with the Virgin Mary, the Apostles, and other disciples, not less than 72 in number. On the left, the death and sepulture of the Virgin, with the Apostles, and other figures necessary for the completion of the picture.

On the vault of the tribune, a niche where the host is deposited, a Christ in glory, in the act of ascending, accompanied with angels; on the one hand the Virgin, St. John the Baptist, St. Peter, and St. Paul; and on the other, the people of Parma.

From the base of the painting to the pavement, imitations of marble and bronze, and the pillars to be ornamented in the same manner.

The price stipulated for this great work, was 350 scudi d'oro al sole.

Pungileoni, t. ii, p. 80.

NOTE P ...... *Girolamo Bedoli, surnamed Mazzola.*

Extract from the Agreement between the Fabric Masters of the cathedral of Parma, and Girolamo Mazzola: as interpreted by Doctor Callegari:

" Item sia tenuto esso M. Jeronimo reponere in la capella quel oro gli è già posto per quondam M. Antonio da Correzzo cum li stagnoli, in questo modo, cioè levato via prima

quel oro li era già su li stagnoli reponere tutto
quello sarà necessario a mordente grasso, dando
li signori fabricanti e facendo loro fare li ponti
necessarii, et queste cose per quel pretio e mercede sarà judicato per il reverendo marchese
Jo. Francesco de la Rosa et magnifico marchese Bartolommeo del Prato, et secondo loro
arbitrio."—Pungileoni, t. ii, p. 230.

NOTE Q ...... *employing oil size as the medium
of adhesion, &c.*

It appears to have been frequently the custom with painters, even in later times, to
employ inferior metal in ornamental gilding;
for I am informed by the rev. Mr. Porter, a
native of Italy, resident at Salisbury, that in
the contract made by the late Pope Pius the
6th for regilding the vaults of St. Peter's, one
of the conditions was a clause, that it should
not be done " *à stagnuoli, ma in ori di zec-
chino.*"   The term stagnuoli describes the pre-
paration called in England, Dutch metal.

NOTE R ..... *selected Correggio to paint them.*

The exact period when these pictures were painted is not known ; Pungileoni assigns to them the date of 1532, and grounds his opinion on two entries in the books of private expenses, preserved in the archives of the duke of Mantua. These record a sum of £ 131. 5. 4. as due in 1537 to " Mastro Antonio da Corezo pictor, per adequatio diun suo conto ;" and as these entries are contained in the same page, with a similar memorandum respecting Sebastiano and others, employed in the decoration of the triumphal arches erected in 1530, he assigns the original debt to Correggio to nearly the same period.—Pungileoni, t. ii, p. 246.

On this point, however, it is proper to observe, that Antonio Bernieri, one of the scholars of Correggio, bore also the appellation of Antonio da Correggio, and was at this period in high reputation, and residing at Mantua ; and therefore this entry may have applied to him. At all events, it is too vague to be adduced in evidence.

NOTE S ...... *a Danaë said to be painted by Correggio.*

By some persons it is supposed that the pieces of the Danaë were again collected, and replaced in the same manner as those of the Io; and indeed we find a painting on that subject, ascribed to Correggio, classed among the pictures in the catalogue of the Orleans collection. It was purchased by Mr. Hope, sold after his death, and is now said to be at Paris; but much difference of opinion prevails among the connoisseurs, whether it be an original or a copy.

NOTE T ...... *for the repose of his soul.*

A dì dicto (6 March) per la sepoltura di M. Antonio de Alegro depintore £13   8
A dì 9 che fù il lunedi fù fato lo septimo di M. Antonio di Alegri, depintore...... .... £13   8
A di 10 fù il martedì fù fato il trigesimo del soprascripto...................£13   6

Pungileoni, t. ii, p. 251.

Note U ...... *register of the convent of St.
Giovanni.*

1524. Francesca Letitia filia Antonii de
Allegris de Corriggia et Hieronymæ uxoris
nascitur 6, baptizatur 26 Septemb.

1526. Catharina Lucretia filia Magistri
Antonii de Allegris de Correggio et Hieronymæ
uxoris, nascitur 24 baptizatur 26 Septemb.

1527. Anna Geria filia Antonii de Allegris
et Jacobinæ uxoris, nascitur 3 baptizatur 5
Octob.—Tiraboschi, t. vi, p. 242.

Note X ..... *a legacy of no less than 250
gold ducats.*

Item jure legati et jure institutionis, reliquit
et legavit dictus testator, honestæ juveni Fran-
ciscæ ejus nepoti, et filiæ quondam magistri
Antonii Pictoris, filii legitimi et naturalis prædicti testatoris et olim Dominæ Hieronymæ de
Merlinis, jugalium, scutos ducentum quinqua-

ginta auri, &c.—Ratti.   Abstract of the will
of Pellegrino, dated 19 November, 1538.   p.
182.

————————

NOTE Y ...... *true and almost inimitable effect
of nature.*

We owe some of these observations to Mengs,
who studied the picture, when at the palace of
Madrid, with an attentive and critical eye.

————————

NOTE Z ...... *carried the clear obscure to the
highest perfection.*

Pungileoni conjectures that this Magdalen
was painted by Correggio for the princess of
Correggio, in order to be presented to the emperor.

————————

NOTE AA.

On this subject we also refer the reader to
the works of Mengs, so often quoted, and to
the lectures of West, Fuseli, and Opie, as well
as to the remarks of sir Joshua Reynolds.

CHAP. III.

To investigate the style of Correggio, is to intrude into the province of professors of the art. We shall, therefore, abstain from pronouncing a judgment on contested points, and confine our remarks chiefly to those characteristics, by which he is generally and unequivocally admitted to have been distinguished.

In design, Correggio has been deemed inferior to the great masters of the Roman school, but this charge has been strenuously resisted by his admirer Mengs. In fact, though intimately and accurately acquainted with the human figure, he seems to have studiously rendered design subservient to harmony and grace. These qualities constitute the leading principles of his style, as well as his distinctive excellencies, and predominate equally in his smaller and in his larger compositions, in his cabinet pieces, as well as in his magnificent

cupolas.   His tints, lights, and shadows are so skilfully balanced and
so artfully blended, as to excite in
the mind the pleasing, yet soothing,
sensation, created by the appearance
of the rain-bow, as described by
Ovid :

> " In quo diversi niteant cum mille colores,
> Transitus ipse tamen spectantia lumina fallit ;
> Usque adeó quod tangit Idem est ; tamen ultima
>   distant."   *Met. lib. a.*

> " A thousand colours gild the face of day,
> With sever'd beauties and distinguish'd ray :
> Whilst in their contact they elude the sight,
> And lose distinction in each other's light."

With harmony and grace Correggio
united another characteristic, to which
his pictures owe their striking and
magical effect ; namely, his clear obscure, or disposition of lights and

shades. By his admirable management of these accidents, his
figures are detached from their
ground, seem surrounded with air, and
deceive the eye and the imagination
with the truth and energy of real
life. To produce this illusion in the
highest degree, the light in some of
his finest pictures is purely ideal, as
in the Penitent Magdalen, the Christ
in the Garden, and particularly in
the Nôtte.

The powerful effect of these qualities united, cannot be better exhibited
than in the words of Fuseli :—

" The harmony of Correggio,
though assisted by exquisite hues, was
entirely independent of colour: his
great organ was *chiaro oscuro*, in its
most extensive sense. He succeeded

in uniting the two opposite principles of light and darkness, by imperceptible gradations. The bland light of a globe, gliding through lucid demitints into rich reflected shades, composes the spell which pervades all his performances. The art of painting had exhibited some of the highest efforts of its power ; the sublime conceptions of Michael Angelo, the pathos and expression of Raphael, and the magic tints of Titian : another charm was yet wanting to complete the circle of perfection, and this charm was found in the harmony of Correggio."

But, although the general character of his pencil is marked by harmony, softness, and grace, he manifested one species of boldness, in

which he equalled every other painter,
not excepting Michael Angelo himself.   We allude to his foreshortening,
which he carried to the highest perfection.   This quality he derived
from an intimate acquaintance with
nature, and an accurate knowledge
of anatomy; and though he has frequently displayed it in such a manner
as to create surprise, yet the most
critical observer has never accused
him of exceeding the boundary of
truth, or degenerating into distor-
tion and caricature.

Correggio appears to have delighted
in the expression of the milder passions ; and in those of love, affection,
and tenderness, he is almost without
a rival.   He has discriminated, with
equal felicity, the different shades of

grief; and has beautifully contrasted them in the dead Christ, painted for the church of St. John. It is profound in the Virgin, tender in the Magdalen, and chastened in the third female figure. He has also manifested his power of indicating manly dignity in the St. George; and though he seldom embodies the fiercer passions, he has shewn his ability in that class of expression, by the figure of the executioner, in the Martyrdom of St. Placido, which was copied in the St. Agnes of Domenichino.*

But perhaps the passion which he has represented with the most striking effect, is that of dignified resignation. In the celebrated

---

* Lanzi, t. iv. p. 96.

Ecce Homo, or Christ shewn to the
Multitude, the divine air of meekness
and patient suffering, which he has
given to the Redeemer of mankind,
awakens the sublimest emotions, and
embodies the animated descriptions
of Holy Writ.[B] The same remark
applies with equal truth to the Agony
of Christ in the Garden.

We cannot close our observations on
his powers of expression, without adverting to a beauty which he possessed
exclusively; or, at least, shared only
with Leonardo da Vinci, namely, the
lovely and exquisite smile, which plays
on his female countenances, and which
has been distinguished by the epithet
of the Corrigesque, or the grace of
Correggio. This trait, as difficult to
describe as to imitate, has been hap-

pily indicated by Dante, the father of
Italian Poetry, in his

> " Della bocca il disiato riso."
>
> *Inferno.*

In this rare and fascinating expression, Correggio alone was capable of
discriminating the precise boundary
between grace and affectation, and
his delicate pencil was fully competent to execute the conception of
his mind. His best copyists, even
the Carracci themselves, generally
failed in preserving this original fea-
ture ; and in many modern copies
and engravings, it often degenerates
into mere grimace.[c]

He was skilful in the management
of his drapery, which is grand and
flowing, and not broken into minute

or angular folds.   He was unrivalled
in delineating naked figures, an excellence which he owed to the transparency of his tints, and his accurate
knowledge of the human form.

The poetical spirit, which animates
his compositions, has not been sufficiently lauded, even by his warmest admirers. Without dwelling on the rich-.
ness of his fancy, in his classical subjects, or the fertility of his invention,
in his Cupolas, we may give, by way
of example, a few instances of this
peculiar happiness of thought.   In the
Education of Cupid, he has not only
given plumage to the Mercury and
Cupid, but has poetically marked the
nature of love, and the volatile character of the goddess of pleasure, by the
emblems of wings, and a bow.   In the

Io, he has represented the dominion
of silence and solitude, by depicting
the Stag, the most timid of animals,
as drinking in tranquillity the waters
of the stream." In the Christ in the
Garden, he has happily indicated the
approaching sufferings of the Redeemer, by the incidental display of
the instruments of the passion, partly
illuminated, and partly cast into
shade. Lastly, in the Nótte, where
the light diffused over the piece,
emanates from the child, he has em-
bodied a thought, at once beautiful,
picturesque, and sublime. "This
idea," as Opie observes, "has been
seized with such avidity, and produced so many imitations, that no
one is accused of plagiarism. The
real author is forgotten, and the

public, accustomed to consider this incident as naturally a part of the subject, have long ceased to inquire, when, or by whom, it was invented."[*]

He is said to have employed the rarest and richest colours, which he laid on in a full body, and frequently retouched with the greatest care and attention.[b]

" His colours," says Mengs, " are inferior to none: he profusely used the ultra-marine, in his drapery, in his flesh, and even in his landscape, a circumstance unusual in the works of any other painter, on account of the

---

* Opie's Lectures.

excessive dearness of the colour. His
lakes are peculiarly rich, his white
also is exquisite, and still retains its
original brilliancy." The clearness
and transparency of his colouring, observes another critic, are inimitable,
and stop at that exact medium in
which lies the purity and perfection
of taste. Thus, he excelled in delineating the forms of angels re-
tiring and melting in the surrounding
æther: they seem the inhabitants
of heaven, crayoned in splendour,
pellucid in glory; their clear and
animated tints breathe a divinity,
they float in air, like the skirts of a
passing cloud; they drop from the
skies, like rain through an April sun.*

---

* Webb on the beauties of painting.

> "———— gay creatures of the element
> That in the colours of the rainbow live,
> And play i' the plighted clouds."
>
> Comus, 1: 299.

Notwithstanding the beauty, softness, and enchanting effect of his oil
pieces, it would be unjust to estimate
the merits of Correggio from those
alone; for in some of them his genius
was confined by the nature of the
subject, and in some by the purpose for which they were intended,
namely as altar-pieces, divided into
compartments, and destined for particular situations. To form a proper
conception of his eminent talents, we
ought to carry our view to his great
works in fresco, the two cupolas of
St. John, and the cathedral at Parma.
These, however, we lament to say,
are so far dilapidated and robbed of

their original beauty, as to afford no perfect idea of those magic powers which awakened the delight and admiration of the great masters of his age. But, still, sufficient traces are left, to prove that he fully merited the enthusiastic strain of praise, which has been invariably coupled with his name; and that he is justly entitled to the elevated rank, in which he has been placed with Raphael, Michael Angelo, and Titian.

Albani, himself celebrated for beauty of colouring and delicacy of expression, renders this tribute to his merits: "To those who admire only works rapidly finished, and seek no farther, I would say how poor are the performances of Correggio, Titian, Raphael, and others, which do not exhibit bold strokes of the pencil; because if we examine the paintings of Correggio, they are all blended, and display no strokes, as no pencilling is seen in nature—nature is so exquisitely united, that she is in a manner inimitable, and to approach her is a grace, which has been bestowed on Correggio, Titian, and Raphael alone."

After panegyrising the merits of Titian, he adds in a tone of enthusiasm: "The other was Correggio, who drew his origin from the Terrestrial Paradise, and bringing from thence divine wings, rose to the angelic regions, to excite wonder by the purity and simplicity of his style;

without falling into that artificial taste, which, however beautiful, is far less delightful."

" I went," says Annibal Carracci, in a letter to his cousin Ludovico, " to see the grand Cupola, which you have so often commended to me, and am quite astonished. To observe so large a composition, so well contrived; and seen from below with such great exactness; and at the same time, such judgment, such grace, and a colouring of real flesh, Good God, not Tibaldo[v], not Nicolini[o], nor even I may say, Raphael himself, can be compared with him. I know not how many paintings I have seen this morning; the Ancona or altarpiece of St. John, and St. Catharine, and the Madonna della Scodella going

to Egypt, and I swear, I would
change none of these for the St. Cecilia.* To speak of the grace of this
St. Catharine, who so gracefully lays
her head on the feet of the beautiful
little Saviour; is she not more
lovely than the St. Mary Magdalen?
That fine old man St. Jerome, is he
not grander,. and at the same time
more tender than that St. Paul,†
which at first appeared to me a mira-
cle, and now seems like a piece of
wood, it is so hard and sharp. However you must have patience even
for your own Parmegiano, because I
now acknowledge, that I have learnt
from this great man, to imitate all his

---

* A well-known picture by Raphael.

† The figure of St. Paul preaching at Athens, in
one of the Cartoons at Hampton Court.

grace, though at a great distance, for the children of Correggio breathe and smile with such a grace and truth, that one cannot refrain from smiling and enjoying one's self with them."

"I write to my brother that he must come, for he will see things which he could never have believed, —18th April, 1580."

"I have been to the Steccata, and the Zocoli, and have observed what you told me many times, and what I now confess to be true; but I will say, that, to my taste, Parmegiano bears no comparison with Correggio, because the thoughts and conceptions of Correggio were his own, evidently drawn from his own mind, and invented by himself, guided only by the original idea. The others all rest on something not their own; some on models, some on statues or drawings: all the productions of the others are represented as they may be; all of this man as they truly are.

"The opportunities which Agostino wished for, have not occurred; and this appears to me a country, which one never could have believed so totally devoid of good taste and of the delights of a painter, for they do nothing but eat and drink, and make love. I promised to impart to you my sentiments; but I confess I am so confused that it is impossible. I rage and weep, to think of the misfortune of poor Antonio; so great a man,

if indeed he were a man, and not an
angel in the flesh, to be lost here, in a
country where he was unknown, and
though worthy of immortality, here to
die unhappily". He and Titian will
always be my delight; and, if I do
not see the works of the latter at
Venice, I shall not die content.*—
April 28, 1580."

The question has been long agitated
whether Correggio ever visited Rome,
and profited by the study of the antique, and the works of Raphael and
Michael Angelo. On this point the
only historical evidence, which has
been adduced, is a tradition recorded
by father Resta, and said to have been
derived through three generations,

---

* Felsina Pittrice, t. i. p. 355.

from the information of his wife.[1] As an authority so slight and doubtful could not be seriously advanced, his biographers and admirers have sought in his works for more valid traces of the models to which he recurred. Mengs contends that his paintings exhibit proofs of an acquaintance with the antique, and the works of Raphael and Michael Angelo. In the head of the Danaë, he traces a resemblance to that of the Venus de Medicis; and, in the St. Jerome, and Mercury Teaching Cupid to Read, he recognises imitations of the Farnese Hercules and the Apollo Belvidere; he also discovers a resemblance to one of the Children of Niobe, in the young man who endeavours to escape from the soldiers, in the picture representing Christ betrayed in the garden. The countenance of the Magdalen, in the St. Jerome, he considers as an imitation of Raphael; and, in the cupola of the church of St. John, he perceives a similitude to the grand style of Michael Angelo, in the frescos of the Vatican.[x] In corroboration of this opinion, he adduces the sudden change, which is perceived in the style of Correggio, at an early period, as a proof that he must have seen and studied compositions superior to his own. Ratti, the copyist of Mengs, coincides with him in opinion. Lanzi cautiously adopts the same sentiment; and Tiraboschi, after comparing the testimony on both sides, leaves the question thus unsettled: " We cannot decide with certainty that Correggio never visited Rome, and yet there is no argument to prove, that he ever saw that

capital."*   Pungileoni, with superior
advantages of research, pronounces a
contrary decision; and affirms, from
the evidence of a continued series of
unquestionable documents, in which
his presence is mentioned at Parma,
Correggio, and other parts of Lombardy, during a number of years,
that, even if he did visit Rome, his
stay must have been limited to a very
short period.   Finally, this opinion is
corroborated by the assertion of Or-
tensio Landi, who had resided some
time at Correggio; and who, in his
Sette Libri de' Cataloghi, printed at
Venice by Giolito, as early as 1552,
says of our painter, " He was a noble
production of nature, rather than of
any master: he died young without

---

* Tiraboschi, t. vi. p. 252.

having been able to see Rome."* Were all other evidence wanting, this testimony of a contemporary, who must have collected his information on the spot, and who published within eighteen years after the death of Correggio, would of itself be decisive.

His occasional imitation of the antique we are not disposed to question; but this admission is far from justifying the inference, that he actually visited Rome; for, in the collections of Mantegna at Mantua, he must have found numerous copies of the antique, and in those of Isabella d'Este, ·and the Ducal Gallery, statues, busts, and relievos, sufficient to gratify his curiosity, and improve his taste. With

---

* Pungileoni, t. ii. p. 103.

N

great deference also to the opinion of Mengs, we have been unable to trace, in the paintings of Correggio, which have fallen under our observation, such striking imitations of Michael Angelo and Raphael, as would countenance the conclusion, that he must have studied and copied their works. In style and character, on the contrary, he widely differed from those two great painters; and, in the tone of colouring, as well as in the science of clear obscure, which were his great characteristics, they were comparatively inferior.

If indeed he imitated the productions of any other pencil, we should rather seek for his models, in the works of Leonardo da Vinci, from whom he may have caught the first principle of clear obscure, and whom he rivals in the graces of his children, and the ineffable smile of the female countenance. We find also a similitude in the fullness, richness, and transparency of his colouring, to that of Giorgione, the imitator of Leonardo, from whom the Venetian school derived its characteristic excellence. We can scarcely doubt, likewise, that he studied in the works of Titian, then in the height of his fame, those tints which approach the animation of real life, and that magic of colouring, which fascinates and almost deceives the sight.[L] These three painters had all attained the perfection of their art at a period anterior to the striking change which marks the best style of Correggio, and their performances he might have found in many parts of Lombardy. To their several excellencies he united his own superior knowledge of anatomy, and unrivalled command of the clear obscure."

With this view of the subject, we shall lay little stress on the anecdote so often repeated, that on seeing one of the pictures of Raphael, Correggio attentively examined it for a considerable time, and then exclaimed, "I am also a painter." This tale rests on a foundation as slight as the thrice-re-repeated tradition derived from his wife, and merits the censure which it has received from Tiraboschi, " as a popular and uncertain report, unworthy the notice of an exact historian."

We cannot close this sketch without a few additional remarks, on a point, which has occasioned great controversy—namely, the question relative to the real circumstances and situation of Correggio.

Vasari has recorded a tradition, that he died in extreme poverty, and the victim of pecuniary distress. He states that, having received at Parma a payment of sixty crowns, which was churlishly made to him in copper, he walked to Correggio with this load, from anxiety to relieve the wants of his family. The weather being extremely sultry, he refreshed himself with cold water, when thus heated with exercise, and was consequently seized with an inflammatory fever, which hurried him to the grave in a few days. This account of Vasari carries internal evidence of its own falsehood. It is, in the first place, related as a mere hearsay, a "si dice"; and it is grounded on a principle, which shews an imperfect acquaintance with the circumstances of Correggio. Vasari lays great stress on the privations which he suffered from the burthen of his family, as if it was numerous; whereas, Correggio never had more than *four* children, *two* of whom did not survive him; and the eldest, Pomponio, was only in his fourteenth year, at the time of his father's death. He likewise adds, that Correggio had reduced himself to extreme misery by continual saving; which, if admitted, would furnish a strong argument against his pretended poverty. Lastly, the sum which he states to have been paid in copper, must have considerably exceeded two hundred weight, a load which no man *could* have carried on foot, the distance of several miles.

This tale is therefore now justly exploded, though an impression still remains, justified in some measure by the remark of Annibal Carracci, (see p. 175) that Correggio lived neglected, and died in indigence. In this, however, as in many other cases, opinion has gone beyond the truth. That he was not so well known and so liberally rewarded, as Raphael, Titian, Michael Angelo, Julio Romano, or even some inferior painters, will not admit of an argument; but, that he lived in obscurity, and was meanly remunerated for all his works, is disproved by a brief review of the facts which we have related. An obscure painter would not have been so frequently employed by rich convents: an obscure painter would not have been selected to decorate the cupolas of the church of St. John and the cathedral at Parma; nor would an obscure painter have been commissioned by a Duke of Mantua, to execute pictures, intended as a present for an Emperor, when two such celebrated masters as Titian and Julio Romano were at hand. We readily admit, that for some of his pieces the remuneration, as recorded, appears inadequate; but, for his larger works, we have a scale of comparison, in the sums paid to other painters, which enables us to decide, that he was as liberally rewarded, as could have been expected, in his situation and circumstances. Thus, while Correggio received 472 gold ducats for his works in the church of St. John, and agreed for 1000 ducats to decorate the cupola and other parts of the cathedral, Raphael had obtained, according to Mengs, 1200 crowns of gold, or 800 ducats for each room of the Vatican,[*] which, considering the difference in the value of money at the capital and at Parma, the fame of Raphael, as the first painter of the age, and the well-known liberality of the popes, is not so disproportionate a recompense, as would justify the inference, that the talents of Correggio were greatly undervalued. But we have a still more satisfactory criterion, in the sums paid to other painters, employed in the same place, and at the same period. For the sou-

---

[*] Mengs, v. iii. p. 9.

thern chapel of the cathedral of Parma, Anselmi was to receive not more than 200 gold ducats; and for the large chapel, only 120 were assigned to Rondani. For the northern chapel, Parmegiano was promised 145 ducats; and even after this painter had improved his style, and increased his reputation, at Rome and Bologna, he engaged to paint the vault of the Capella Maggiore, in the church of the Steccata at Parma, for the sum of 400 gold crowns. The subject, according to the sketch still preserved, was to be the Coronation of the Virgin, with many groups of angels, and numerous other figures; and those which are actually finished, attest the grandeur of the original design. We may also adduce the instance of Costa, who is called " eximio pittore", and who received for a picture of Apollo and the Nine Muses 30 ducats; and to the elder Dosso, for a large picture, with eleven figures, the same sum was paid. Both these painters, are mentioned in the preceding pages as having served as models to Correggio, while at Mantua, and as being patronised by the princes of that illustrious house.

The researches of his later biographers have not only disproved the tale of his extreme indigence and obscurity, but have brought to light many facts, which enable us to form a more accurate judgment of the real circumstances of his family. We have shewn that he obtained some property by the gift of his uncle, and that he received a respectable dowry with his wife. Pungileoni also asserts, on the authority of indubitable documents, that his family possessions continued to increase, from 1526 till the period of his death. The same writer has adduced two proofs, that subsequent to the suspension of his labours in the cathedral, Correggio was not involved in pecuniary distress; for, in 1531, soon after the last payment, which he received from that establishment, a record has been found of a purchase which he made from Signora Lucrezia Pusterla, of Mantua, widow of a citizen of Correggio, of some landed property, situated in the Campagna del Ardione; the price was 195 crowns of gold, of which 95 were paid in advance. As late also as the autumn of 1533, we find evidence of another purchase, of landed property, from Leonardo Gardini, only a few months before his decease.

Lastly, the registers of notaries, and valuations of property, preserved in the public records at Correggio, prove, that at the very period of his death, the effects of his father, besides personal property, consisted of 206 acres of land, which, at the value of 10 ducats each, amounted to 2060 ducats. He possessed also four houses in the city of Correggio, and he had doubtless made other acquisitions, of which no record is extant.[*]

We farther find proofs, that so far from being unknown and neglected, he was favoured by his native princes, particularly Manfredo; and, from the fact of his being selected as a witness to acts executed in their palace,

---

[*] Pungileoni, t. ii. p. 276.

and in which they were personally concerned, we are fully justified in inferring, that he was treated by them with the utmost familiarity and intimacy. Thus, without dwelling on other instances, in 1532 he attested the instrument by which Manfredo constituted Pomponio Brunorio his procurator, to receive from the Emperor the investiture of his fiefs; and in 1534, a short period before his decease, he attended as a witness to the acts relative to the marriage, between Clara of Correggio and Ippolito, son of Gilberto, by Veronica Gambara. Manfredo, his patron, also personally interfered in the long-pending law-suit between him and the Aromani, and by his interposition, brought it to a conclusion favourable to his interests. From these data, and from the inheritance which devolved on his son Pomponio, it is evident, that Correggio could not have lived in embarrassment and died in poverty.

Correggio appears to have been far less solicitous than most other painters, that his effigies should be transmitted to posterity, for of him there is no unquestioned portrait extant. That which is prefixed to his Life, in the Roman edition of Vasari, is evidently false, for it exhibits the beard and countenance of a man aged seventy. It was taken from a collection of designs, in the possession of Father Resta, to one of which, representing a man and his wife, with *three sons* and one daughter, in mean apparel, he gave the name of the family of Correggio, forgetting that the family consisted of *three* daughters and *one* son.*

Another portrait, with the title Antonius Correggius, and consequently supposed to be painted by himself, was preserved in a villa, which belonged to the Queen of Sardinia, near Turin, and engraved by Valperga; but its authenticity seems justly questioned by Lanzi and Pungileoni. A third, which was sent from Genoa to England, bore an inscription signifying that it was the portrait of Maestro Antonio da Correggio, by Dosso Dossi, and was accordingly engraved for the Memoirs of Correggio, by Ratti, who obtained a copy. Lanzi is however inclined to infer that it is the portrait

------

* Lanzi.

of Antonio Bernieri, the miniature painter, who also bore the name of Antonio da Correggio.

A copy of this portrait is still preserved in the Pinacotheca Bodoniana, at Parma, and has been engraved, first by Asioli, and since as a medallion, by Professor Rocca, of Reggio. Pungileoni, who is inclined to consider it as genuine, has prefixed the medallion to his life of Correggio.

Tiraboschi and Pungileoni mention other supposed portraits and busts of questionable authenticity; and Pungileoni, in particular, adverts to a portrait still preserved near a door of the Cathedral at Parma, which is exhibited as a likeness of Correggio. It is supposed to have been copied in the middle of the sixteenth century, by Lattanzio Gambara, from a more ancient one of our celebrated painter, in another part of the Cathedral; but its authenticity is questioned, merely on the ground, that it represents a man of more advanced age than Correggio, who only attained his forty-first year. The portrait, however, as appears from an accurate copy by Mr. Jackson, R.A., does not warrant these doubts of its genuineness, for it displays no character of an age more advanced, than the period of life which Correggio attained. It is, therefore, engraved for the frontispiece to these pages, as possessing at least as good a title to authenticity as any of the portraits extant.

Pomponio Quirino, the only son of Antonio, was born in 1521, and baptised at the Basilica of St. Quirino, in Correggio, on the third day of September.[o] Inspired by the skill and reputation of his father, he embraced the same profession, but could have acquired from him little more than the elements of his art, as he had not reached the age of thirteen at his decease. He probably continued the practice of painting under some of his father's scholars, and in 1542, on the death of his grandfather, Pellegrino, became heir to considerable property. Soon afterwards, he espoused Laura, daughter of Ludovico Geminiano, with whom he had a dowry of 300 golden crowns. The favour which the princes of Correggio had bestowed on his father, was transferred to him; for, by the influence of Manfredo, he was declared competent to the management of his property, before he had attained the age of twenty-five, the legitimate period of majority in Italy. In the latter end of 1545, he received a still greater proof of attention; for the illustrious spouse of Prince Ippolito, from respect to the memory of his father, condescended to be godmother on the baptism of his first son. In 1546, we find the first proof of the exercise of his profession, in a fresco which he executed for the price of 50 gold crowns, in the Basilica of St. Quirino. Unlike his father, he appears to have been of a profuse and unsettled disposition. In 1550 he sold his paternal mansion to Bernardino Paris, for the sum of 109 gold crowns; and, after disposing at different times of other portions of his property, in 1551 he alienated the remainder to the canons

of St. Quirino for 700 gold crowns.
Even in these transactions, he still ex-
perienced the favour of his sovereigns;
the transfer, which was contrary to
the customs of the country, being
legalised by the special decision of
Prince Gilberto.   After a short sojourn
at Reggio, he settled at Parma, and
was employed to paint the Capella
dei Popoli, by the canons of the cathedral, from whom he received 80 crowns
of gold.   He subsequently engaged in
other works, yet appears to have gradually declined in his circumstances,
from his careless and dissipated habits.
He lost his wife in 1560, but he himself lived beyond 1590, as he is mentioned in that year as an arbitrator, on
a painting executed by Giambattista
Tinti, for the confraternity of St. Maria
degli Angeli.   We have no means of

ascertaining his rank as a painter,
though he has evidently suffered in
public opinion, by a comparison of his
works with those of his father; but the
subjects of his pencil and the persons
by whom he was employed, suffice to
shew, that he was not without reputation in his time.   He had two sons
and three daughters, four of whom
survived him, and are distinguished in
the testamentary bequest of their maternal uncle, Ludovico Geminiano,[p] by
a legacy of an hundred gold crowns to
each.   In the sons of Pomponio the
male line of Correggio became extinct,
and we have no evidence to ascertain
whether his grand-daughters were
married and left issue.   At all events,
by the dissipation of Pomponio, the
family appear to have sunk into obscurity.   In the female line the race

is equally extinct, for Francesca, the daughter of Antonio, and the wife of Pomponio Brunorio, died at the age of forty-seven, without issue.

The fame of Antonio Allegri gave a new impulse to the art of painting in Lombardy; and, though he seems to have instructed few or no regular scholars, he is placed at the head of the Lombard school. Francesco Maria Mazzola, usually known by the appellations of Parmegiano, or Parmegianino,* is supposed to have been one of his scholars, though without foundation, as he had distinguished himself before Correggio went to Parma. Another of the same family, Francesco Maria Rondani, called also Parme-

---

* See the next article.

giano, because he was a native of that city, has been ranked as his scholar, with still less reason; for he was born in the latter end of the same century, and when Correggio appeared at Parma, had reached the age of eighteen and obtained a considerable portion of celebrity. He, however, wrought under him at the church of St. John, and so far profited by his works and instructions, that some of his paintings have been mistaken for those of our great master. He was engaged to paint a large chapel at the same time. He died in 1548.

Anselmi has been enumerated among his scholars, with even less probability, for he was born at Sienna in 1491, and was therefore three years older than Correggio. Of him, however, it may be equally said, that he greatly profited by the works of Correggio, and imitated him with the same felicity as Rondani. He appears to have been living in 1554.

Bernardino Gatti, surnamed Il Sojaro, is one of those whom without hesitation we may term a scholar of Correggio. He was born about the beginning of the sixteenth century; and, after receiving the first rudiments of his art at Sienna, repaired to Parma, for the instructions of Correggio, when in the commencement of his reputation. He is justly regarded as the most faithful and ablest imitator of his master, and has left many proofs of his talents at Parma, Placentia, and Cremona. The cupola of the Steccata at Parma,

in particular, furnishes evidence of his
extraordinary merit. He died in 1571.

Another of his scholars, was Georgio Gandini, a native of Parma. Of
his pencil we have no certain production; but the estimation in which he
was held by his countrymen, is proved
by the choice made of him, by the
canons of the cathedral, to finish the
work left incomplete by Correggio.
He died young in 1538.

Antonio Bernieri, a native of Correggio, and descended from a noble
family, was born in 1516. He was
instructed by his illustrious countryman, but afterwards devoted himself
to miniature painting, in which he attained great celebrity. He is often
distinguished by the name of Antonio

da Correggio, and hence has given rise to many mistakes in the accounts of biographers.   He died in 1565.

To these may be added Lelio Orsi, born at Reggio in 1511, and called Da Novellara, from his early residence in that city.   Whether a scholar of Correggio or not is uncertain ; but he appears to have derived great advantage from the study of his compositions, and to have combined the grace and clear obscure of Correggio, with the bold design of Michael Angelo. In particular, he made a copy of the celebrated Nótte, which is said almost to rival the original.   He wrought chiefly in Reggio and Modena, and died in 1587.*

---

* Ticozzi—Ratti, p. 136.

One painter, though not a scholar of this distinguished master, deserves to be here commemorated, as an admirer and copier of his works, and as an imitator of his style. This was Girolamo Carpi, a native of Ferrara, and son of an heraldic painter. Having acquired a taste for the arts, under Benvenuto Cellini, he became impatient of the mechanical labours to which he was subjected by his father, and, quitting his home, repaired to Bologna. Here he was struck by the picture of Christ appearing to Mary Magdalen,[q] in the likeness of the gardener, by Correggio; and endeavoured to improve his style, by copying this production. From Bologna he was led to Modena, by the same motive, and there copied the Marriage of St. Catharine, the celebrated St. George, or St. Pietro Martire, and the no less celebrated St. Sebastian. Thence he repaired to Parma, to study the magnificent works in the church of St. John and the cathedral, of many parts of which he also made copies, particularly of the Virgin ascending to Heaven, the Apostles and Doctors of the Church, and the accompanying groupes of angels. By this species of practice, his style and taste were much improved; and, though he afterwards studied the works of Raphael, Titian, and Parmegiano, he chiefly confined his imitations to the great example he had first chosen.

He became a painter of considerable eminence, and left many performances, both in his native place and at Bologna and Rome. Afterwards, devoting himself to architecture, he was

employed at Rome by Pope Julius III.
and, on returning to his native country, was gratified with the patronage
of his sovereign, Hercules, third Duke
of Ferrara. According to Vasari, he
died in 1556, at the age of fifty-five.
He was so accurate an imitator, that
some of his copies have been taken for
the originals of Correggio.[*]

Francesco Capelli, Giovanni Garolo,
Antonio Bruno, Daniello da Por, and
Maestro Torelli, or Tonelli, are enumerated, not as scholars of Correggio,
but as having either wrought under
his directions, or improved themselves
by the study of his works. Of these
painters, however, few productions
remain, and most of them questionable;

---

[*] Vasari, t. v. p. 311.

and of their lives, very few facts have been rescued from oblivion. We shall, therefore, here close our remarks, as we think it needless to enumerate every one who imitated the style of Correggio, and shall merely observe, that, after his death, the reputation of the Lombard school was ably supported by Parmegiano, his coadjutors, and followers. It is, however, a fact, acknowledged by all judges of the art, that no painter has since attained the admirable grace, clear obscure, and harmony, which characterise the works of Correggio, as no succeeding painter has been enabled to rival the exquisite pathos and noble simplicity of Raphael.

NOTES TO CHAP. III.

NOTE A ...... *disposition of lights and shades.*

MUCH confusion has been thrown on this subject, by the adoption of the foreign term *chiaroscuro*, or clear obscure, as we translate it; when the simple words light and shade, would convey all the meaning which that term is intended to express. Its effect cannot be better illustrated, than by adverting to the appearance of a bunch of grapes, illuminated by rays of light, which Titian is said to have used as a pattern. As some of the grapes are struck directly by the light, others thrown into shade, and some partake of both, partly from the direct rays, and partly from reflection, they furnish an apt exemplification of the manner in which the lights and shades aid and animate the disposition of a groupe of figures in painting.

P

Note B ...... *the animated descriptions of Holy Writ.*

Two pictures of the Ecce Homo are extant, with strong claims to authenticity; one is in the Royal Gallery of France, and is supposed to have been derived from the family of Prati, at Parma; and the other was in the Colonna Palace, at Rome, in 1786, and appears to possess superior pretensions to originality. Tiraboschi, t. vi. p. 284, and Voyage d'un Amateur des Arts, t. iv, p. 279.

Note C ...... *often degenerates into mere grimace.*

One of the modern copyists of Correggio, who may be exempted from this disqualification, was Guttenbrun, a German artist of considerable eminence, now dead. He was happy in his imitations of this master, of which he has left many proofs. Among others, is a beautiful copy of the Marriage of St. Catherine, at Naples, which is in the collection of Count Woronzoff; and another, exquisitely finished, on a small scale, of the Virgin and Child, in the Nótte, in the possession of the Countess of Pembroke, at Wilton House.

We must likewise make another honourable exception, in favour of Mr. Jackson, R. A., who has so admirably copied the picture of the Agony of Christ in the Garden.

———

Note D ...... *the waters of the stream.*

An Io, attributed to Correggio, is preserved in the Imperial Gallery at Vienna, in which the stag is depicted as drinking from an antique vase, and not from a rivulet. This absurd representation essentially changes the character of the piece, and suffices to throw discredit on its authenticity as a work of Correggio, who was so attentive to character, and so accurate an observer of nature.

Gemaelde der K. K. Gallerie, 1 part, p. 171.

NOTE E. ...... *and frequently retouched with the greatest care and attention.*

In describing the colouring of Correggio, it may not be improper to record the observations of an artist on his mode of operation. We give these remarks as related by Lanzi :—

"An artist, who analyzed his mode of colouring, said, that he washed the gisso, or first coat, with boiled oil, on which he painted with a strong impasto, or full body of colour, mixing it with two-thirds of oil and one of varnish. Ilis colours must have been choice, and purged of saline matter, which in process of time greatly injures all paintings. This purification was increased by the use of the boiled oil, which absorbed the salts. He farther conjectured, that Correggio warmed his pictures in the sun, or by the fire, to blend and mingle his colours together, as they appear rather melted than laid on. Of their transparency, he was inclined to attribute the cause, to a varnish, more powerful than any known even to the Flemish painters, whose varnishes are clear and shining, but not equally strong."—Lanzi, t. v. p. 84. note.

The Richardsons supposed that he used a priming of leaf gold. Pungileoni partly coincides with them, with respect to his early pictures, as, in the Madonna and Child, preserved in the Gallery at Dresden, some threads of gold leaf are observable in the extremities of the garments, as well as in another picture, which he calls the St. Martha. But, he concludes, that he afterwards employed a composition known only to himself, and that he invented a varnish, which gave a peculiar lustre and transparency to his tints, t. ii. p. 35.

It is also mentioned, as a proof of his solicitude to attain perfection, that the material on which his pictures are painted, whether of canvas or wood, is always of a superior kind.

NOTE F ...... *not Tibaldo.*

He alludes to Tibaldi Pellegrino, born at Bologna in 1522, and one of the eminent painters of the Roman school.

NOTE G ...... *not Nicolini.*

Probably, Nicolo Abate, a painter of the
Bolognese school, who was distinguished for his
happy imitations of Raphael and Correggio.
He was born in 1512; and, after exercising his
art with great applause in his native city, repaired to France in 1552, and decorated the
Royal Palace of Fontainebleau with paintings
in fresco.

NOTE H ...... *here to die unhappily.*

These expressions evidently refer to Correggio,
who is called by his Christian name, Antonio;
and prove that, either from the writings of
Vasari, or from traditional report, Annibal Carracci considered him as ill patronized by his
countrymen, poor in his circumstances, and un-
fortunate in his death.

NOTE I ...... *the information of his wife.*

This hearsay of a hearsay is said to have been told by the wife of Correggio to her anonymous friend, Signora N. N. who died at the age of ninety.   This lady related it to another female friend, who lived to an advanced age, and she retailed it in her turn to Signora Ottaviana Donini, who is declared to have frequently mentioned it to Father Resta, when in 1690 he repaired to Correggio, to obtain information on the life of this great painter.   Tiraboschi, t. vi, p. 251.

NOTE K ...... *in the frescos of the Vatican.*

This remark of Mengs cannot apply, as some have supposed, to the celebrated fresco of the Last Judgment, in the Sestini Chapel, by Michael Angelo, because that work could not have been commenced before the death of Correggio, as it was not begun till after the accession of Paul III. in 1534, and not finished

till 1541.   In fact, the only fresco of Michael
Angelo completed at an earlier period, was the
ceiling of the same chapel, in 1512.

NOTE L ...... *that magic of colouring, which
fascinates and almost deceives the sight.*

Some critics have supposed that Correggio
owed an improvement in his style to the works
of Julio Romano, which he might have seen at
Mantua.   By a comparison of dates and facts,
however, it appears that Correggio must have
attained his best style, before Julio Romano engaged in the service of the Duke of Mantua,
and long before he executed the celebrated frescos in the Palace of the T.; for Julio could not
have left Rome earlier than 1525 or 1526; and
the Palace of the T. of which he was the architect, could scarcely have been sufficiently advanced to receive its decorations, before 1530 or
1531.

NOTE M ...... *unrivalled command of the clear obscure.*

Mengs gives many examples of a corresponding character, between the productions of Leonardo da Vinci and Correggio, which he considers as proofs of imitation. We have already noticed the head of the Madonna, now in the Gallery of Dresden, as resembling those of Leonardo; and Mengs, after adverting to the graceful and smiling air of some children, in two paintings by that master, at Madrid, adds, " these may have opened the way to Correggio to attain that grace which we see in all his works." As Raphael, likewise, admired and imitated the compositions of Leonardo, and caught from him that improvement, which marks his most perfect style, we may readily account for the similarities which have been supposed to exist between some of his works and those of Correggio, without concluding that Correggio must have visited Rome.

NOTE N ...... *for each room of the Vatican.*

It is well known, that the paintings, executed by Raphael in the Vatican, cover the
four sides of the apartments, which are very
lofty, and without fire-places or furniture.
Some are crowded with figures, particularly the
Incendio del Borgo, and the Victory of Constantine over Maxentius.   The School of
Athens, which occupies only the end of one
apartment, contains no less than fifty-eight
figures, of the size of life.   The Attila, and
the Deliverance of St. Peter from Prison,
appear to have employed Raphael and his scholars at least two years, namely, from 1512,
when the Heliodorus was completed, to
1514.

NOTE O ...... *on the third day of September.*

His baptism is thus recorded in the Register :
" Pomponius Quirinus, fil. Antonii de Allegris,
die 3. 7bris 1521, Compatr. Mag. Joan Bap-
tista de Lombardis; Comater . . . . . de Fássis.
Pungileoni, t. iii. p. 60.

———————

NOTE P ......*their maternal uncle, Ludovico*
Geminiano.

Extract from the Will of Ludovico Geminiano: " Item jure legati reliquit Hieronyme et
Sulpiciæ fil. D. Pomponii de Allegris et D.
Lauræ, scutos centum pro quolibet earum dan-
dos * * * quando maritabuntur * * * Item jure
legati reliquit Antonio et Pompilio filiis D.
Pomponii et qm. D. Lauræ scutos centum pro
quolibet ipsorum. Pungileoni, t. ii. p. 265.

NOTE Q .... *the picture of Christ appearing
to Mary Magdalen.*

This picture, when copied by Carpi, was in
the possession of the Ercolani family. Tiraboschi conjectures that it was conveyed to Spain
by the Duke of Medina de las Torres; and
Mengs informs us, that in his time it was preserved in the grand vestry of the Escurial.
It probably remains there, as it does not appear
to have been among those purloined by Joseph
Buonaparte.   A picture, however, on the same
subject, ascribed to Correggio, was preserved in
the collection of the Duke of Orleans.

BIOGRAPHICAL SKETCH

OF

FRANCESCO MAZZOLA,

SURNAMED

PARMEGIANO.

INTRODUCTION.

Almost as many errors abound in the account of Girolamo Francesco Maria Mazzola, usually denominated Parmegiano, and Parmegianino, as in that of Correggio. His pictures are often confounded with those of Francesco Maria Rondani, and of his cousin, Girolamo Mazzola, who both bore the designation of Parmegiano. These mistakes have principally arisen from the identity of their birth-place, and

the similarity of their appellatives;
although, to avoid such confusion, our
painter omitted his first name of Giro-.
lamo, and always signed Francesco.
His talents have thus been often
undeservedly depreciated; for his two
relatives were inferior in merit, and
strikingly differed from him in one
peculiarity, namely, that of filling
their canvass with figures; whereas,
his field is never crowded to the
disadvantage of his subject.

These errors have been exposed
and corrected by Father Affò, his biographer, Vice Prefect of the Royal
Library at Parma, in a work intituled
" Vita del Graziosissimo Pittore, Francesco Mazzola, detto il Parmegiani-

no." Parma, 1784, octavo. This is the most authentic account extant, and has furnished the principal materials for the following sketch.*

---

* It is but justice to Mr. Bryan to observe, that, in his Dictionary of Painters, he has judiciously availed himself, as far as his limits would permit, of Affò's work.

PARMEGIANO.

CHAP. I.

GIROLAMO Francesco Maria Mazzola was born at Parma, and from

that place derived the appellations by
which he is usually distinguished. By
foreigners, he is termed Parmegiano,
or the Parmesan; while, among his
own countrymen, he has been distinguished by the endearing diminutive
Parmegianino, as expressive of the
amiable qualities of his mind and person, or as indicating the grace and
elegance of his pencil. He was descended from an ancient family originally of Pontremoli, some of whom were
settled at Parma as early as 1305. Of
this family were three painters, sons
of Bartholomeo Mazzola; namely—
Philippo, Michele, and Pietro Ilario,
moderate in their kind, but who have
had the honour of being reputed masters of Correggio; though, as Tiraboschi shews, without sufficient foundation. An indifferent painting by Phi-

lippo is still preserved at Parma, Christ Baptised in the Jordan by John the Baptist, with this inscription: "Ppus Mazzolus, pt." Pietro Ilario painted as late as 1515, and was employed in the church of St. John at Parma. But Philippo was of greater service to the art, in being father to the celebrated painter, who is the subject of this narrative.

Various opinions are held of the year of his birth; some even fix it in 1515, an evident error, as, on this supposition he could not have exceeded his twelfth year, when he was engaged to paint, in conjunction with Correggio and others, the church of St. John at Parma. Others say he was born in 1500. Vasari, who knew his cousin, Girolamo, fixed his birth in 1504.

From the baptismal register, however, it appears that he was born on the 11th of January, 1503, and baptised on the 13th, by the names of Girolamo Francesco Maria. His father dying when he was young, he came under the care of his uncles and guardians, Michele and Pietro Ilario. He received a classical education in his native city, and was intended for one of the learned professions; but, though not deficient. in application to his studies, he paid greater attention to the easels of his uncles, and when not engaged at school, employed himself in designing. Observing the natural taste of their nephew, his uncles prudently instructed him in the art of painting. From them he learned the first principles of design, but doubtless received instructions, or at least improved himself, by studying the compositions of Francesco Marmitta, a native of Parma, and esteemed, at that period, the best painter of the place.*   He is also, with some probability, said to have been the scholar of Taddeo Ugoleto, who seems to have been another master of eminence at Parma.   Notwithstanding, however, his attachment to painting, he does not seem to have neglected his other studies, particularly history, mythology, and natural philosophy, as sufcient proofs of his progress in these branches of knowledge appear in his works.   He was esteemed by his con-

---

* Marmitta afterwards distinguished himself as an engraver of gems. Abecedario Pittorico, p. 316.—Some persons have asserted that Marmitta died in 1506, and therefore could not have instructed Parmegiano.

temporaries a youth of a bold and lively
genius, yet of courteous and elegant
manners. He is generally supposed to
have been the scholar of Correggio, or
at least to have formed his *early* style
from that great master. But this opinion is contradicted by *facts;* for, at
the age of fourteen, before Correggio
came to Parma, Mazzola had distinguished himself by painting the Baptism of Christ, which was much admired, and in which that grace and
elegant lightness, afterwards conspicuous in his works, were visible. This
picture was first placed in the church
of the Annunziata at Parma; but, towards the end of the last century, it
was, according to the information of
Lanzi, possessed by the Counts of San
Vitale. Soon after this period, also,
the war which broke out between

Francis the First, and Pope Leo the Tenth in Lombardy; and the approach of a body of Papal troops to Parma, induced his uncles to send him and his cousin, Girolamo, to Viadano, in the territory of Mantua, where, Vasari says, Francesco Mazzola painted two celebrated pieces, a St. Francis, for the Franciscan church, and the Espousals of St. Catharine, for that of St. Peter, not resembling, he adds, the works of a beginner and a youth, but of a master and a proficient. In 1522, he returned to Parma, where his compositions raised him to great notice; for, according to Vasari, he finished some pieces, which he had left imperfect at his departure; and, among others, a beautiful painting in oil, representing the Virgin with the child on her bosom, attended by St.

Jerome and St. Bernardino di Feltre.*
Although he had scarcely completed
his twentieth year, he was, from such
striking indications of merit, subsequently selected to decorate the sides
and roof of two chapels near the en-
trance of the church of St. John, while
Correggio was engaged in painting
the dome. Several other of his labours are still preserved at Parma, and
indicate his style, when he had seen
the works of Correggio, but not those
of Raphael and Michael Angelo.

He gave so much satisfaction in
these performances, that he was engaged to paint the sides and roof of a

---

* Affò observes, that, in his time, this picture was
preserved in the chapel of the Dormitory, belonging to
the church of the Annunciation.

chapel in the cathedral, in conjunction with Rondani, while Correggio was preparing to ornament the cupola and choir; and the nave was consigned to Alessandro Araldi.* The note of the contract made Nov. 21, 1522, is still preserved, in Italian, in his own hand, as well as the instrument itself, by which he agreed to execute four figures in the divisions of the ceiling of the Chapel, north of the Dome, in which the altar of the Nativity was situated, together with other decorations. He was to finish his work in the same style as that adopted for the neighbouring Chapel, and to receive 145 ducats of gold, the Chapter providing scaffolding and other requisites. As he was still a minor, his

---

* Pungileoni, t. i. p. 213.

two uncles, Michele, and Pietro Ilario,
were witnesses and securities. His
cousin Rondani was to receive at the
same time, 120 ducats of gold for
painting another part of the Church;
and Michael Angelo Anselmi, for decorating a third Chapel, on the south,
the sum of 200. But Mazzola never
commenced his engagement, because
it was dependent on certain altera-
tions to be made in the Cathedral,
and on the termination of the labours
of Correggio, in the Church of St.
John, which did not occur till about
1524. Indeed as it was not resumed
at a subsequent period, it was probably cancelled by mutual consent.

During this interval, Mazzola seems
to have felt, that in imitating the style
of any single master, however excel-

lent, he should fail to attain that eminence to which he aspired.   The reputation of Raphael and Michael Angelo awakened his curiosity and emu-
lation, and he formed the resolution
of contemplating the·productions of
the Roman school, which presented
a new and peculiar character of grandeur and grace, united with correctness of design.   He therefore took his
departure in 1523 from Parma, at the
age of twenty, in company with his
uncle Michele.   With the hope of ob-
taining the patronage of Clement 7th,
who had recently succeeded to the
papal chair, he carried with him three
pictures, which he had finished ex-
pressly to procure an introduction to
his Holiness.

The largest of these represented the
Virgin with the child on her bosom,

taking fruit from the lap of an angel. Another was intended to exhibit a striking specimen of pictorial illusion. It was a portrait of himself, delineated on a convex surface of wood, exactly representing the appearance displayed by a mirror. The figure of the artist, as well as the furniture and windows of the chamber, in which he was supposed to sit, were so artfully depicted, and so happily imitated, that the whole appeared as if reflected from a polished or glassy surface. Vasari, who saw it, observes, that as he was of a comely form, his countenance more resembling an Angel than a man, his effigies thus exhibited, appeared something divine. This picture, after passing through several hands, particularly those of the celebrated Aretino, where it was admired by Vasari, was said by Bottari in his notes on that Author, to be finally deposited in the Treasury at Vienna.

Mazzola was well received by the Pope. Although his Holiness was accustomed to the excellent compositions of Raphael, he was much struck with the works of the young stranger, made him several presents, and gave him great encouragement to deserve his patronage. To manifest his gratitude for the praises and rewards, which he obtained from the Papal court, Parmegiano presented to the Pope a picture, which proves his knowledge of the clear obscure, an excellence which he had caught from the masterly designs of Correggio. The subject was the Circumcision of Christ, and it was remarkable for the introduction of three different lights, without affecting the general harmony. The figures in the foreground were irradiated from the infant Jesus, the second series from torches in the hands of persons, bringing sacrificial gifts; and the back ground was a pleasing landscape, enlightened by the early dawn. This piece which was much valued by the Pope, was afterwards in possession of the emperor Charles the Fifth.

During his continuance at Rome, Parmegiano studied with the utmost diligence the antique, and the works of the most celebrated painters; but particularly those of Raphael, Michael Angelo, and Julio Romano. Of Raphael especially, he imitated the style and manner, and as he resembled that painter in beauty of countenance and elegance of deportment, it was currently said, that the soul of Raphael had emigrated into the body of Parmegiano.   He now added to his other acquisitions the study of anatomy, and proved the delicacy of his taste, by avoiding the prominent defect of Michael Angelo, who was reproached with too great a display of anatomical knowledge.   In fact he now formed the style, which was peculiarly his own, and which has been said to unite the characteristics of Raphael, Michael Angelo, and Correggio.

He expected to be employed in painting the Hall of the Vatican, which John of Udina had already stuccoed and divided into compartments for the purpose; but his hopes were fatally disappointed, by the progress of hostilities between the Emperor and the Pope, for the blockade and siege of Rome absorbed the atten-

tion of Clement, and superseded the
cultivation of the Arts.

During his short stay at Rome, Vasari says, he painted several small
pictures, most of which became the
property of the Cardinal Ippolito de'
Medici. Of his larger works, the
biographer specifies three; a round
picture of the Annunciation, which he
praises as singularly beautiful, and
which was painted for M. Agnolo
Cesis; a picture of our Lady and
Christ, with several Angels and a St.
Joseph, remarkable for the pleasing
air of the heads, the beauty of the
colouring, and the grace and skill with
which it is finished; and a portrait of
Signor Lorenzo Cibò, captain of the
papal guard, which was said to be
equal to life itself. Finally he was

engaged to paint a picture for Madonna Maria Buffalina da Città di Castello, which was intended to be placed in the Church of St. Salvatore del Lauro. It represented the Virgin in the clouds, holding a book, with the child on her knees; St. John kneeling on the earth, and St. Jerome asleep at a distance; and from this figure it is styled the Vision of St. Jerome.[A]

While he was engaged in this performance, the memorable sack of Rome, in 1527 occurred, and an anecdote is recorded of him, similar to that which is related of Protogenes the Greek painter, during the siege of Rhodes by Demetrius. In consequence of his fixed attention to this work, he neither heard the roaring of the cannon, nor perceived the

tumult of the assault, till some soldiers rushed into his apartment, and
surprised him in the midst of his
labours.

Fortunately, the chief of the troop,
who entered his room, was a man of
taste, and being much struck with his
compositions, checked the rapacity of
his followers, and exacted from the
painter, only some sketches in pen
and ink, with which he was highly
gratified.

Another party more regardless of
the arts, insisting on money, he went
out to borrow a sum from a friend,
when he was seized by a third troop,
by whom he was imprisoned, until he
had found means to satisfy their demands.

A city recently sacked, and filled with foreign troops, being an insecure residence for an artist, he retired to Bologna, where he lodged in the house of a saddler, his countryman and friend, and proposed to remain for a time, with the view of etching his best compositions, the art of engraving on copper having been recently discovered.

During his residence at Rome, Parmegiano is said to have invented the Chiaroscuro [B] method of engraving on wood; and a print of his own Diogenes, in that style, is falsely attributed to him, for it was done by Hugo de Carpi, the inventor of that method, whose name appears at the bottom of the impression. Some also ascribe to him the invention of

etching on copper, and others of mez-
zotinto ; but both without foundation.
He seems, however, to have been
among the first who introduced etching into Italy, and to have greatly
improved the art. During his residence at Bologna, he not only made
many etchings of his own works,
which were much admired, but employed a skilful artist, named Bernardo da Trento, to engrave others.
He was at length diverted from his
pursuit, by the treachery of Bernardo
who decamped, after stealing his
tools and designs. In consequence
of this loss, he resumed the pencil,
and painted many pictures for different individuals, and convents.
Among these are enumerated a St.
Roque, attacked with the plague; a
Conversion of St. Paul, with numerous

figures, a Landscape, and a Madonna of great beauty, for his host the saddler. Indeed several of his most esteemed pieces were executed in that city, and it is singular, that during so short a stay, his pencil should have been so wonderfully productive.

One particularly distinguished for its beauty, was that called the Madonna della Rosa, which represents the Virgin in the act of offering a Rose to the infant Jesus, who rests his hand on the globe. Of this picture a curious anecdote is related. It is said to have been executed for the celebrated Aretino, who was on terms of friendship with the painter; and critics who have examined it minutely, have discovered faint traces

of wings on the shoulders of the infant, ornaments on the female, and
other proofs, that the original design,
was a Venus and Cupid, which was
certainly more consonant to the character of the licentious satyrist, than
a religious subject. Some suppose,
however, that the painter changed his
purpose, and having thus transformed
it, presented it to Pope Clement 7th,
and others that it was sold to the
family of Zani, at Bologna; in whose
possession it continued till 1752, when
it was purchased by Augustus the
Third, King of Poland and Elector
of Saxony, for the price of 1,350 zecchines, and now adorns the gallery
at Dresden.*   It is painted on wood,

---

* Affo, and Description de la Gallerie de Dresde.

and in dimensions is four french feet,
by three feet 2 inches.*

Another was the celebrated picture
called the Madonna del Collo Lungo.
It represents the Virgin, with the infant Jesus, sleeping in her lap, accompanied with a group of Angels, one of
whom holds a transparent vase, containing the figure of an illuminated
cross. It was executed for the Church
of Sta. Maria de' Servi, and afterwards sold by the monks to Cosmo
the Third, great duke of Florence, who
placed it in the Pitti Palace, and
substituted a copy in the church.
This proceeding occasioned a process
between the Marchese Cerati, the
patron of the Church, and the Monks,

---

* Abregé de la Vie des Peintres, p. 135, Affò.

but as the original was irrecoverable, he deprived them of their copy.[c]

Lastly the celebrated altar-piece of the Convent of St. Margaret, deserves particular attention. It exhibits the Virgin presenting the infant Jesus to St. Margaret the Martyr, and near are the figures of St. Benedict, and St. Jerome, with an Angel. It was greatly admired, and studied by the Carracci; and Scaramucci relates, that Guido being asked by a friend, which he would prefer, this picture or the St. Cecilia of Raphael, exclaimed after a long pause, in a transport of enthusiasm " Quella, quella di Santa Margaretta del Parmegianino."[a]

---

[a] Oh, by all means this; this of St. Margaret by Parmegianino !

Parmegiano entertained a high opinion of his profession, and was extremely jealous of his reputation; for he never permitted any picture to go out of his hands, till quite finished. An instance of his punctilious delicacy is recorded by his biographer at this period. The emperor Charles the Fifth being crowned at Bologna by Pope Clement the seventh, Parmegiano, after witnessing the ceremony, drew from memory his portrait crowned by fame, with a boy in the character of an infant Hercules, offering him the globe. The Pope, who was much delighted with the sketch, sent it to the Emperor, who was no less pleased, and desired to retain it; but the artist excused himself, because it was unfinished. In a short time Charles departed from Bologna,

and Parmegiano thus lost the patronage which he otherwise might have
obtained from the Emperor. The portrait when finished, was preṣented to
the Pope, inherited by his nephew,
Cardinal de' Medici, and afterwards
transferred to the gallery of Mantua,
where it probably perished in the
memorable sack of that city, in
1630.

NOTES TO CHAP. I.

Note A ...... *the Vision of St. Jerome.*

Vasari says, the picture painted for Donna Maria Buffalini, was intended to be placed in the Church of St. Salvatore del Lauro, in a chapel near the door. He adds that when Parmegiano left Rome, he deposited it with the Frati della Pace, in whose refectory it remained several years. It was removed by Giulio Buffalini to the church of the family at Città di Castello.

Affò, after relating these facts, adds that it remained in the refectory of the monastery of St. Maria della Pace, till the time when Biondo wrote; that it was removed by Giulio Buffalini, and doubtless placed in the chapel of that noble family, in the church of the Augustins. But in consequence of the little care which was taken of it, the Buffalini family caused it to be transferred to their palace, in which it remained in his (Affò's) time, and though considerably injured, was regarded as a treasure.

This picture was purchased by the late Marquess of Abercorn, who sold it to Watson Taylor, esq., at his sale it has been recently purchased by the Reverend Holwell Carr, at the price of 3,050 guineas.

NOTE II ...... *the Chiaroscuro Method of Engraving.*

THIS mode of printing was performed first by means of two, and afterwards of three blocks of wood. In the first mode the shades and outline were impressed with one block, the tints of colour with a second, and the lights were left blank. In the second mode, one block was employed for shade and outline, a second for the middle, and a third for the bright tints; and the lights, as before, were generally left blank. Vasari, t. iv, p. 284.

NOTE C ...... *deprived them of their copy.*

Ratti, p. 150.   Affò, p. 75, states that he saw and examined it in 1782, at the house of Signor Guasti, whither it was removed during the repairs of the church.   It is now in the Ducal Gallery at Florence.

CHAP. II.

<hr>

AFTER having increased his reputation and improved his taste at Rome and Bologna, Parmegiano was eager to display his talents in his native

city.   He accordingly returned to
Parma in 1531, and was instantly engaged to paint the principal chapel
in the church of La Steccata, dedicated
to the Virgin Mary, and then recently
built.

Having made a design, which
represented the coronation of the
Virgin, surrounded with groupes of
Angels, it was approved by the fraternity, and he contracted to paint
the Chapel in fresco, for 400 gold
crowns, to be finished in 18 months.
In the following year he received half
the payment in advance.   Some delays in erecting the scaffolding, which
was to be furnished by the fraternity,
however induced Parmegiano to employ himself in decorating a ceiling
for the family of San Vitali, at their

palace of Fontanalato. The subject
was the story of Acteon; the light
was derived from a torch, in the
hands of a female figure; and a representation of Ceres was deemed not
unworthy of the pencil of Correggio.
He was also engaged in other pictures, particularly portraits, in which
he greatly excelled.

In these occupations he passed four
years, without fulfilling his contract
with the fraternity; but in compliance
with their remonstrances he signed
a new deed, on the 27th of September,
1535, engaging to finish the work in
two years, under pain of forfeiting
the payment. He at the same time
received a new advance of fifty gold
crowns, Francis Boiardi and Damiano

Piazza being his sureties for fulfilling
the agreement.

In gratitude to Boiardi, he painted
for him a beautiful picture, the subject of which is Cupid forming a
bow. The God of Love is represented
with his back towards the spectator,
the right-foot resting on some books,
and the face partly turned to the
front. In the back ground is a small
Cupid, embracing a girl, whose attitude evinces alarm and timidity.
These subordinate figures are sweetly
and naturally depicted, and the expression and attitude of Cupid himself, is in the highest degree characteristic, elegant, and graceful.

We cannot pay a greater compliment to the merits of Parmegiano, than by stating that this picture has been attributed to Correggio, and as such is enumerated in the catalogue of the Imperial Gallery at Vienna, where it now remains. It has also been engraved by Francis Vanderstein as a production of Correggio.

This picture was celebrated at an early period; for soon after the death of the painter, we find Francesco Doria writing to his friend Carnesecchi, and recommending him when at Parma to examine the Cupid of Parmegianino, then in the possession of the Cavalier Boiardi. According to Vasari, it descended by inheritance, with other designs of our painter, to Marcantonio Cavalea, the grandson of Boiardi, and was afterwards supposed to have been

carried into Spain, and to have formed
one of the ornaments of the Escurial.
Whether this was the fact, or by what
means it came into the possession of
the emperor, is equally uncertain;
though it may have passed as a present from the court of Madrid to that
of Vienna, during the intimate con-
nection between the two branches of
the House of Austria.*

Another picture of the same character, justly attributed to Parmegiano,
is preserved in the collection of Capo
di Monte at Naples.   It represents
Cupid asleep and two genii archly

---

* Gemælde der K. K. Gallerie, p. 1, p. 170. The
editor of this Catalogue states, that the picture has
been injured, particularly the body of the Cupid, though
the head is still perfect.

attempting to steal his bow; and displays all the playful elegance of his pencil.[*]

After executing several other works, which were no less admired, he commenced his labours in the church of La Steccata, and completed the beautiful figures of Adam and Eve, the three Virgins, by some called Sibylls; Moses breaking the tables of the law, so much and justly admired; and the ornaments in the vault of the presbytery. He proceeded, however, with extreme dilatoriness, and was almost continually engaged in executing private commissions. Some attribute his delays to a dread of having his fresco paintings compared with those of Correggio, in the Churches of St. John and the Cathedral; others with

* Voyage d' un Amateur des Arts, t. iii. p. 36.

Vasari, to his pursuit of the philosopher's stone, but this imputation is
disproved, by the testimony of his
friend and scholar Fornari.[*]   Some
also ascribe them to a propensity for
gaming; adding, that vexed with the
loss of a large sum of money at play,
he ascended the scaffolding, and defaced great part of his performance.

Affò has vindicated him from both
these imputations.   Most probably
his delays arose from his profuse and
improvident temper; for having dissipated the sums which he received
from the fraternity, he was compelled
for subsistence to engage in those
works, which would yield him a ready
supply of money.   But whatever was
the cause of his neglect, he was

____

* Affò, p. 87.

arrested and imprisoned, for not fulfilling his contract. This disgrace
filled him with disgust and melancholy,
though to obtain his liberty, he seems
to have promised to complete the
work. But soon after his release he
escaped to Casal Maggiore, in the
territory of Cremona, where he for a
short time continued his labours, and
painted two pieces, which proved that
the vigour of his pencil was undiminished. These were, a valuable picture
for the Church of St. Francis, of which
the subject is not specified, and another, as an altar piece for the Collegiate
Church, representing the Virgin in
the Clouds, and beneath St. John and
St. Stephen. To this period is also
ascribed the Lucretia, meditating her
death, with the poignard in her hand,
which for expression and force, as

well as purity of design, is called by
Vasari the most exquisite of his productions.[A]

He did not, however, long survive
his liberation from prison, for he was
seized with a violent fever, which
hurried him to the grave, on the
24th of August, 1540, in his 37th
year, dying by a singular coin-
cidence at the same age as his
favourite prototype the inimitable
Raphael. His body, at his own re-
quest, was removed from Casal Maggiore, and interred in the Church of
the convent of Fontana, naked, with
a cross of cypress laid on the breast.
Being unmarried, and without children, he left a testament, constituting
three of his friends as his heirs, to
the exclusion of his own relations.

Against them a law-suit was speedily instituted, by the confraternity of La Steccata, to obtain compensation for the non-fulfilment of his contract. They defended the omission, on the ground, that his employers had failed to furnish the leaf gold required for the work, and to remove and dispose the scaffoldings; but after a valuation of the part which was finished, they were enjoined to reimburse the convent, by the payment of 150 Imperial lire.[B]

The style of Parmegiano is evidently grounded on that of Correggio, though he successfully superadded the characteristics of Raphael and Michael Angelo. He is however far removed from the reproach of servile imitation, and though he has so ad-

mirably blended their respective
beauties, his style is exclusively his
own. His chief object was delicacy
and elegance, which he has evinced
in the air of his female figures, the
contrasts of his attitudes, and the easy
flow of his drapery.

He is indeed reproached as a man-
nerist, for carrying these peculiarities
to excess; and particularly in his
zealous imitation of the antique, is
said to have made the extremities of
his female forms, too slender for the
proportions of natural beauty. This
defect is remarked in one of his
finest figures, which is thence called
the Madonna del Collo lungo, or long-
necked Madonna. But although he
may in some degree merit the censure of sacrificing such essentials to

ideal elegance, he has fully proved his ability to attain sublimity and dignity. Of this, many proofs may be drawn from his works in fresco, and particularly from his celebrated figure of Moses breaking the tables of the law, which is highly impressive, for the character of the head, the majesty of the form, and the energy and dignity of the attitude. Of this figure, Sir Joshua Reynolds observes, we are at a loss which to admire most, the correctness of the drawing, or the grandeur of the conception. It furnished also to one of our most celebrated lyric poets, the no less animated description of the British Bard:

> On a rock whose haughty brow
> Frowns o'er old Conway's foaming flood,
> Robed in the sable garb of Woe,
> With haggard eyes the poet stood.

Loose his *beard* and *hoary hair*,
Stream'd like a meteor to the troubled air ;
And with a master's hand and prophet's fire,
Struck the deep sorrows of his lyre.*

Among the excellencies of Parmegiano, we may enumerate the appropriate and harmonious tone of his colouring ; and may equally commend the judicious arrangement of his subjects ; for he generally abstained from crowding his field, and was thus enabled to give his figures their due proportion and full effect. Indeed almost the only composition mentioned by his biographers, as departing from this rule, is " Christ preaching to the Multitude," which was preserved in the Villa of Colorno belonging to the sovereigns of Parma.† Another ex-

---

* Mason's Edition of Gray, v. 4.

† Lanzi, t. iv, p. 101.

cellence was his skill and accuracy in
design, in which he has been justly
compared with Raphael. So ambi-
tious was he of perfection in this
branch of art, that he is said to have
made repeated draughts of his principal figures; and of the Adam in the
Steccata, in particular, no less than
three different sketches have been
discovered and engraved. Hence he
is said to have been slow and deli-
berate in his conceptions; forming
his plan with great care, before he
took up the pencil; and then finish-
ing his work, with that freedom and
decision, which called forth so warm
and enthusiastic an eulogium from
Albani.

" Bold touches," says that able
master, " justly given in the proper

place, are highly to be commended,
as the great Parmegiano has shewn.
In this respect he was a prodigy of
nature, sent into the world by
Heaven, to awaken the wonder of
mankind; for by the frequent practice of design, he had so far acquired
this habit, that when he passed from
the conception of his subject to the
exercise of the pencil, his touches
were divine."*

Parmegiano seems to have left
still fewer scholars than Correggio.
Indeed his errant mode of life must
have afforded little opportunity for
giving regular instruction; and none
of his biographers attempt to assign
to him any other pupil than his cousin

---

* Felsina Pittrice, t. iv, p. 249.

Girolamo Mazzola, who though a painter of some merit, was considerably inferior, and whose performances, as we have already observed, have been sometimes mistaken for those of Parmegiano.

T

NOTES TO CHAP. II.

Note A ...... *and Scholar Fornari.*

Affò attributes the tale of his devotion to Alchemy, to the invention of ignorant observers, who seeing him employed with crucibles in preparing his colours, supposed him engaged in the pursuit of the philosopher's stone. The imputation of a propensity to gaming, is traced to a ridiculous mistake of the abbé Richard, in the Description Historique de l' Italie. Finding the following expression in Sandrart " Pergebat autem in supradicto quidem opere fornicis, sed tarduis, quod seposita aliquando pictura alchimiæ dedisset operam: cum autem una die plus perderet quam integra hebdomada lucraretur, &c." he considered the word ' perderet' as applied to gaming, and, in consequence, not only accused him of having lost a consider-able sum at play, but added that in a fit of

vexation he defaced a part of his work, and fled
to Casal Maggiore.   The first of these imputations is, as Affò observes, an obvious error;
and the second is fully disproved by the records
of the lawsuit with his executors, in which
such a fact would have been infallibly adduced,
in order to establish the claim for damages set
up by the confraternity of the Steccata.   Affò,
p. 99.

NOTE B ...... *the most exquisite of his productions.*

This Lucretia is supposed to be lost, though
one by Parmegiano on the same subject is
enumerated in the *Descrizione di cento quadri,*
preserved in the Farnese Gallery, printed in
1725.   These pictures were afterwards transferred to the palace of Capo di Monte at
Naples.   Like the celebrated Cupid, the Lucretia has also been ascribed to Correggio.—
Affò, p. 89.—Voyage d'un Amateur des Arts.
t. iv, p. 32.

Note C. ...... *by the payment of* 150 *Imperial lire.*

This sum did not exceed thirty-eight gold crowns, which is an additional proof of the falsity of the assertion, that Parmegiano had destroyed the greater part of his performance; since the work, according to the contract, was to be completed for 400, and he received in part 250. The portion which he had finished, must therefore have been valued at 212, and consequently, the money refunded, was not more than one sixth of the whole advance.

INDEX.

INDEX.

INDEX.

INDEX.

INDEX.

S.

T.

INDEX.

T. C. Hansard, Printer,
Peterborough-court, Fleet-street.